THE MURDER CABINET

Roger Keevil

The Inspector Constable Murder Mysteries

Murderer's Fête
Murder Unearthed
Death Sails In The Sunset
Murder Comes To Call
Murder Most Frequent
The Odds On Murder
The Murder Cabinet

THE MURDER CABINET

by
Roger Keevil

THE MURDER CABINET

an Inspector Constable murder mystery

by

Roger Keevil

Copyright © 2017 Roger Keevil

The moral right of the author has been asserted.

Apart from any fair dealing for the purposes of research or private study, or criticism or review, as permitted under the Copyright, Designs and Patents Act 1988, this publication may only be reproduced, stored or transmitted, in any form or by any means, with the prior permission of the publisher, or in the case of reprographic reproduction in accordance with the terms of licences issued by the Copyright Licensing Agency. Enquiries concerning reproduction outside these terms should be sent to the publisher.

mail@rogerkeevil.co.uk
www.rogerkeevil.co.uk

'The Murder Cabinet' is a work of fiction and wholly the product of the imagination of the author. All persons, events, locations, and organisations are entirely fictitious or are used fictitiously, and are not intended to resemble in any way any actual persons living or dead, events, locations or organisations. Any such resemblance is entirely coincidental, and is wholly in the mind of the reader.

But you knew that already, didn't you?

To the person who first suggested to me that
Inspector Constable and Sergeant Copper should
appear in print,
and to the many loyal readers who have followed
them over the years,
this book, with my grateful thanks, is dedicated.

"In my beginning is my end"

Printed by CreateSpace, An Amazon.com
company
Available on Kindle and other devices

Chapter 1

"Bit of a cliché, isn't it, sir?" remarked Detective Sergeant Dave Copper.

"Mmmm?" absently responded Detective Inspector Andy Constable, his attention focussed on the dead body lying before him.

"A politician getting stabbed in the back, guv. I mean, we know journalists talk about it all the time ..."

"But you don't expect that you're actually going to see one in real life. So to speak."

"And I certainly never expected to be back in here." Copper looked around the room at the bookshelves lining the walls. "With an actual body in the room this time."

"I seem to remember your rather flat-footed attempt at humour on our last visit." Constable smiled grimly. "Which went down like a lead balloon."

Copper frowned. "So who on earth is going to be Prime Minister now, guv?"

"That, sergeant, is one thing we do not have to trouble ourselves with, thank goodness," replied Constable. "I suspect we shall have enough to do, finding out who killed this one." He took a deep breath. "Well, I suppose we'd better make a start."

*

Andy Constable stood in the doorway to his office, supporting himself with both hands against the door jamb. His face bore an expression of stunned bemusement which Dave Copper had never seen before in all the years they'd worked together.

"So what's the Lawless situation then, guv?" asked Copper brightly.

"That's Chief Superintendent Lawless to you, sergeant," retorted Constable. "You haven't got your promotion yet. And this is not the occasion for levity."

"Sorry, sir." Copper sounded chastened. "So what's afoot, guv?" enquired the sergeant, puzzled. "I'd hardly had a chance to get behind my desk first thing when we get sudden demands from the Chief Super for your immediate attendance, as close to yesterday as possible. I don't think she was too impressed when I said you'd gone to the loo. Maybe she doesn't think you ought to be doing that sort of thing on police time. And she wouldn't say what it was about. It all sounds very mysterious."

"And it's going to remain that way, as far as everyone else is concerned." Constable shook himself slightly, and his voice filled with determination. "Right. Get your jacket on. You and me, and not a word to anyone else for the time being. I'll fill you in when we're in the car. We're off to Dammett Hall."

"Hell's bells!" ejaculated Copper, as the two detectives headed down the corridor towards the police station car park. "That brings back memories. It's a few years since we got called out there, isn't it? Don't tell me they've been at it again at Château Lawdown?"

"It doesn't belong to the Lawdowns any more," explained Constable over his shoulder. "Not for a while now."

"I remember the money side of things wasn't too good when we were there on that other case," mused Copper. "So what did they do – flog it off?"

"Something like that, I gather. There was an article about it in the paper which caught my eye, just because I noticed the name. And probably the business with the murder didn't make it the happiest place to live. So somebody bought it and turned it into a country house hotel." Constable blipped the car door locks and the detectives climbed in.

"And having had one murder there, somebody thought it would be great fun to have another one. Is that it, guv?" grinned Copper.

"Yes, there's been another murder," replied Constable grimly. He directed a brief sideways glance at his junior colleague. "But you do not find me smiling."

"Oh, come on, guv," said Copper. "Take pity on a poor bewildered sergeant. What on earth is going on?"

"This absolutely goes no further for now, until I know what we're facing. All I know is, it's the P.M."

"Blimey!" responded Copper. "That's jumping the gun a bit, isn't it? They don't normally get on with the post-mortem before we've at least had a chance to look at the body."

"Not that p.m.," said Constable with a touch

of asperity. "*The* P.M. - the Prime Minister." He took a deep breath. "She's been killed."

"What!?!"

"You heard. The Prime Minister of the United Kingdom has been killed."

"What, murdered?" Copper was aghast. "Sorry, sir – stupid question. Of course it's murder – why else would we be on our way there? But ... why us, for goodness sake? I mean, wouldn't the Prime Minister be up to her ears in police and security and whatnot?"

"You'd think so. But in this instance, apparently not. So somebody somewhere is probably going to catch a very severe cold when this is all over. But for the time being, the whole thing is being kept under very tight wraps. Something to do with not announcing anything while the European stock markets are still open. Somebody extremely high up has leaned very heavily on the Police and Crime Commissioner, who has leaned on the Chief Constable, who has leaned on the Chief Super, who had nowhere to go but lucky old us. And since we knew the Dammett Hall turf from the previous case ..."

"As you say, guv, lucky old us."

"We have the rest of the day to sort out what we can. After that, the whole thing goes public, and the big battalions rush in."

"No pressure then, sir."

"None at all," agreed Constable with a taut smile.

"Guv," ventured Copper after a brief and reflective silence. "Sorry to sound stupid, but I don't get it. I mean, you know me and politics. I don't follow them at all. So you'd better help me out with a bit of background, or else I'm only going to show you up when we start asking questions."

Constable sighed. "Another tutorial? I should have gone into teaching. Oh well – it'll fill the time till we get there."

*

The previous two years in British politics had certainly lived up to the ancient Chinese curse about living in interesting times. Following a controversial result in a referendum about a major issue concerning the country's future, a general election called to resolve the matter had ended up with an even more confusing picture. Massive recriminations followed, and all the major parties were convulsed with a period of bitter in-fighting which led to the dissolution of many old allegiances and the forming of some surprising new ones. Favourites to succeed to the party leaderships rose and fell with breathtaking swiftness. Freshly-formed parties, some of them coalitions of people from every part of the political spectrum, emerged, and in the second general election which followed swiftly on the heels of the first, the Alternative Alliance Party swept unexpectedly to power. Headed by its charismatic leader, Doris Ronson, former mayor of a major northern city, the party held an overwhelming majority in Parliament, although its claim to be bringing an entirely new face to British politics was somewhat belied by the number of familiar faces from several of the old parties who now occupied the seats around the Cabinet table.

As Britain's third woman Prime Minister, Doris Ronson was a godsend to the media. Dubbed 'Diamond Doris' by the tabloids – to those who loved her, the title was an accolade as the female 'diamond geezer' of the masses, whereas to those who loathed her, it was a condemnation of her resolutely adamant stance in certain areas of policy – she was instantly recognisable, with her mop of unwillingly-tamed grey-blonde hair, her trademark trouser suits in a startling range of colours, and her businesslike bustling walk.

"So what's she doing at Dammett Hall?" asked Copper. "Do prime ministers often go off to country house hotels? And you said there was nothing in the way of security. Please don't tell me she'd sneaked off for a naughty weekend."

"From what I gather," replied Constable, declining to react to his colleague's implication, "it was supposed to be a secret meeting of a group of ministers away from the prying eyes of the TV and press. Some sort of unofficial inner cabinet, I think. But don't ask me exactly why – apparently there are wheels within wheels, and everybody is being very tight-lipped about the whole thing."

"I still can't figure out why Dammett Hall, guv. I mean, prime ministers have got their own official country house for this sort of thing, haven't they? So why couldn't they use

Chequers?"

"Death Watch Beetle in the timbers, I believe. I'm told half the roof's off, so for some reason they picked Dammett Hall as a suitably discreet alternative venue."

"Putting us on our very own death watch. Great!"

"Copper," said Constable severely, "I suggest that in the context of the situation, you make strenuous efforts to keep your well-known sense of humour under rigid control. People may not be as understanding as I, lord help me, have had to be over the years."

"Right, guv. Sorry, guv," responded Copper humbly. "So who's running the country while all this is going on?"

"The Deputy Prime Minister, I gather. He's probably sat behind a desk in Downing Street at this very moment with his head in his hands waiting for us to tell him what's been going on. So, let's not disappoint."

After passing through the village of Dammett Worthy, it only took a minute or two to reach the gates of Dammett Hall, where the car was halted by a familiar uniformed figure standing in the opening.

Constable lowered his window. "Well, well. Collins, isn't it?"

"That's right, sir. Fancy you remembering me after all this while," smiled Robbie Collins.

"I'm hardly likely to have forgotten our last meeting," said the inspector. "Although I notice a set of stripes that wasn't there when I was here before. Congratulations on the promotion."

"Thank you, sir," said Sergeant Collins. "Well, I won't hold you up. You'll be wanting to get on up to the house. I was told to expect you, although I don't really know what's going on. Some sort of trouble up there, they said, and nobody's to get past me without authority. Oh, and I'm to expect the police doctor as well." A speculative look entered his eye. "So does that mean ...?"

"Let's just say, Collins," replied Constable, "that it seems that you and I are fated to be brought together again by the discovery of a dead body at the Hall. And you didn't hear that from me."

"Right you are, sir. Understood." Collins stepped back and gave a smart salute as the detectives' car pulled past him and headed up the drive, past the sign in elegant lettering reading 'Dammett Hall Country House Hotel'.

As the house came into sight, Andy Constable reflected that Dammett Hall appeared completely unchanged from his first visit. The soft red brickwork with its accents of creamy grey stone at the corners, the dormer windows, the cluster of tall chimneys, all still exuded an air of unruffled calm. The lone monumental cedar still graced the sweep of lawn which fell to the lake. But at the foot of the steps which led to the front door sat the familiar prime-ministerial limousine, with a formidable black security SUV in attendance. At the sound of the approaching car, a female figure appeared at the front door of the Hall and descended the steps to greet the new arrivals. She appeared to be in her mid-forties, with a sturdy build and grey-brown hair cut in a short business-like style. Her dark grey suit was well-tailored, and her shoes of the kind best described as sensible.

"Inspector Constable?" She held out her hand as the detectives emerged from the car. "How do you do? Thank you for getting here so quickly. I'm Sheila Deare – head of the P.M.'s security detail."

Constable shook the proffered hand. "How do you do, Miss ... Mrs ...?"

"Inspector. But call me Sheila, please."

"Andy."

"Andrew?"

"Andy," reiterated Constable firmly. "And this is my colleague, Sergeant David Copper. You'd better call him sergeant, or else he'll start getting ideas above his station. Although having said that, you may not have the chance to call him sergeant much longer, if the results of a certain set of exams come through. So, what's all this about?"

Sheila's reply was forestalled by the sound of a further set of wheels crunching on the gravel of the drive, as a rather battered-looking Volvo estate drew to a halt alongside the detectives' vehicle, and a plump jolly-looking man climbed out.

"Andy!" he cried in greeting. "I have the strangest sense of déja-vu!"

"Morning, doc," said Constable. "We meet

yet again. But yes, I'm afraid Dammett Hall is apparently hosting another dead body which requires your attention."

"Not in the garden again by any chance?" asked the doctor. "If so, I think I can remember the way."

Constable raised his eyebrows in enquiry. "Inspector ... Sheila?"

"No, doctor. The ... er ... the victim is in the library."

The doctor mounted the steps to the front door. "Which I take it will be through here and ..."

"Third door on the right," chorused the detectives in unison, before sharing a wry grin.

"I'd better get on, then," said the doctor. "You coming, Andy?"

"Be with you in a second, doc. I need to talk to Inspector Deare here to find out more about the current set-up."

"And do we have any idea who the victim is?"

"Oh yes, doc," replied Constable heavily. "We do. You'll soon see." He declined to say any more and, with a frown and a slight shrug, the doctor disappeared into the house.

"We may as well go inside as well," said Sheila, following in the doctor's wake and stopping in the centre of the hall. "I don't know where you want to begin. I've got the man who found the body – he's the general manager of the hotel, and he's stashed away on his own in his office. And it all happened before any of the ministers had come down for breakfast, so I've got them all to stay in their own rooms for the time being. That's pretty much it. There's been nobody else in the house since last night."

"What, no staff? In a place this size?"

"Normally there would be, yes, but the P.M. wanted as few people around as possible, so other than me, there's just one chap from the Number 10 catering staff."

"And you weren't staying in the house?" Constable was incredulous. "I'd have thought that, as the P.M.'s security officer, you'd have stuck to her like glue."

"And so I would normally," replied Sheila Deare, "but orders were, nobody but the P.M. and the ministers at the house last night, and there weren't any spare bedrooms available here anyway, so the P.M.'s driver, the waiter and I stayed overnight at the pub in the village. The driver's still down at the pub - the waiter and I arrived this morning at pretty much the same time as the general manager appeared, and he was the first one into the library where he found Mrs. Ronson."

"At which point, no doubt, all hell broke loose?" surmised Constable.

"Absolutely not," retorted Sheila firmly. "We can't afford to panic in this business. So the waiter was sent into the kitchen with strict orders to stay put, the manager's in his office in the old butler's pantry as I said, the ministers are all upstairs, and I was on to my boss at the Met within about five seconds of checking that there wasn't a great deal of point in calling for an ambulance."

"Very organised," said Constable, impressed. "At which point, the wheels of Whitehall began to turn? And, I'm guessing, on this occasion, not exceeding slow."

"Yes. I got a call from the Deputy P.M. within minutes. He put me in total control on the spot, and said that I was to expect someone from the local force. You, in fact."

"And that ended up with the phone on my desk ringing, and here I am. And you reckon everybody's hermetically sealed off? But do they know the Prime Minister's dead?"

"Yes, I told them that. Just that. The bare fact – well, there wasn't much else to tell. Other than the fact that she's obviously been murdered, but I didn't want to reveal even that to them at that stage."

"But surely ..." A thought struck Constable. "You can't keep something like this under wraps. They'll all have been on their phones straight away. I bet this story's all round the world by now."

"I had the hotel manager disconnect all the room phones this morning," said Sheila grimly. "And I'd already taken charge of everyone's mobiles."

"Really?" Constable was astounded. "And the ministers let you have them?"

"P.M.'s orders," replied the security officer shortly. "She was absolutely determined that nothing about this meeting was going to leak, so she ordered them all as soon as they got here yesterday to hand over their phones into my keeping. They didn't like it. Not one little bit. But orders are orders, and I had my job to do. Still do, for that matter. Although whether I will still have a job in twenty-four hours after what's happened is another matter. But until I get a direct order from the top, I'll carry on obeying Mrs. Ronson's instructions."

Constable shook his head in wonder. "So what's all this about? Why are they here in the first place? And why this obsessive level of secrecy?"

"I have no idea. Above my pay grade, I'm afraid. I assume the ministers can tell you."

"I shall have to ask them, shan't I? And we keep talking about them as an amorphous group instead of individuals. I suppose you ought to tell me who they are." Constable turned to his junior. "Copper, you'd better make a list of these. I dare say we're going to have to work our way through them one by one."

"Righty-ho, guv." The sergeant produced his notebook.

Sheila drew a breath. "Right. Well, the most senior is Amanda Laye, the Foreign Secretary. She only got back from a trip yesterday – more or less came here straight from the airport. Then there's the Health Secretary, Dr. Neal – Peregrine Neal, although in these ruthlessly chummy man-of-the-people days he'll probably insist that you call him Perry. Erica Mayall is here – she's the Secretary of State for Women's Affairs." Sheila thought for a moment. "We've got Benjamin Fitt who is Social Security Secretary, and the Education Secretary, Milo Grade. How many's that so far?"

"Five."

"Okay – three more. Deborah Nye is in the group – she's the Justice Secretary, and she's also got her Minister of State with her – that's Marion Hayste, who's the Prisons Minister. And the last on the list would be the Culture and Media Secretary, Lewis Stalker. That's the lot."

"You start to wonder who's running the country," murmured Dave Copper.

"Right," said Constable briskly, declining to acknowledge his colleague's remark. "Sequence of events. What led up to now? How come we are where we are?"

"The P.M. decided to have this meeting," said Sheila. "For whatever reason – I don't get to know things like why. And because of the state of things at Chequers ..."

"Which I've been told about," intervened Constable.

"... she got me to cast around for an alternative venue. I found Dammett Hall, which seemed to fit the bill – small, slightly away from the mainstream, discreet. The ministers all turned up here late on Thursday afternoon ..." Sheila broke off. "Good lord, that's only yesterday. It seems like forever ago. Anyway, they were all here by teatime."

"Did they arrive together? On some sort of ministerial charabanc?"

Sheila smiled faintly. "This lot? Oh no. Far

beneath their dignity. Things like that may be all right for the Royal Family when they're moving en masse to get to Westminster Abbey for a wedding, but it would never do for our grandees. No, everyone came in their own separate official car – oh, except Dee and Marion. Same department, so they came together."

"I get the vague impression that you are not necessarily a huge personal fan of some of these people?" hazarded Constable.

"Totally irrelevant," said Sheila crisply. "I'm a professional – I do the job I'm expected to."

"But no man is a hero to his valet, eh?" suggested Constable. "Well, go on."

"Mrs. Ronson had a brief chat with everybody, and then they had dinner."

"Here?"

"No. The P.M. wanted the staff numbers kept to a minimum, so it was arranged that the party would have dinner at the pub."

"Is that the Dammett Well Inn in the village, by any chance?" asked Constable.

"That's right. They have a private dining room, and the food is actually rather good. I'd eaten there when I checked the place out for accommodation for myself and the others."

"I'd have thought a fleet of ministerial limousines drawing up outside the village pub would have been likely to attract attention," remarked Constable. "Wouldn't that rather tend to scupper the idea of keeping this affair quiet?"

"We cut it down to two," said Sheila. "The P.M. plus four in her car, and me plus four in the escort vehicle. Not too much of a squeeze, and it kept the profile low. Everyone went in through a side door, so Joe Public never caught a glimpse. And apart from the landlord and one of his waitresses, nobody knew about the dinner. The private function room is quite separate from the rest of the Dammett Well."

"Is Gideon Porter still the landlord down there?" enquired Copper.

"Yes," said Sheila. "Do you know him?"

"We met on a previous case," said Copper. He turned to Constable. "Blimey, guv. Old Gideon must have been taking cooking lessons if he's up to catering for the great and the good."

The inspector refused to be diverted from the narrative. "And then?"

"After the meal, everybody came back here, and Mrs. Ronson told all the other ministers' cars to leave, and come back here at six o'clock this evening for the end of the meeting. Then she told me I wouldn't be needed again until this morning, so the driver and the waiter and I were sent off back to the pub, leaving the ministers here alone. And that was all I knew until I arrived back here this morning."

Constable let out a gusty sigh. "Right. Well, that puts me in the picture up to that point. As for what went on after that, I shall have to talk to all the others. And I'm going to need a SOCO team up here as soon as possible."

Sheila shook her head. "Sorry, Andy. Absolutely not. At least, not yet. This whole thing is limited to those people on the premises until this evening. Strict instructions from the Chancellor – this is not to get out."

"But why ...?" Constable remembered. "Because of the effect on the markets. Of course. Okay – so we're on our own. And now I suppose we'd better go and have a look at the scene of the crime."

As Constable led the way towards the library door, it opened and the doctor emerged. "Well, Andy," he said, "I have to say that, in a lifetime of surprises, you've never presented me with a bigger one than this." He shook his head in incredulity. "The Prime Minister, for goodness sake? Talk about ending your career with a bang."

"So she's been shot?"

"Not her, man! Me!"

Constable frowned. "I don't understand."

"Nobody's got around to telling you? Typical!" tutted the doctor. "The ones who need to know are always the last ones to find out. I'm retiring. This is supposed to be my last day. Although the chances of me getting away with that now look pretty remote. I seem to have acquired an unscheduled appointment with a highly-placed corpse in my dissecting room."

"You retire, doc?" Andy Constable was disbelieving. "Never. How on earth would we manage without you?"

"Anno domini gets us all in the end, Andy." He glanced over his shoulder towards the room he had just left. "That's if some malefactor doesn't beat us to it."

"We shall be sorry to see you go, doc. Truly."

"Anyway," said the doctor, clearing his throat gruffly at the hint of emotion in the air, "back to business. And no, she hasn't been shot. It's a very simple single stab wound, inflicted from the rear, straight to the heart. Death probably instantaneous, and some hours ago, but I can't be too exact on that without a more detailed examination. As for the weapon, there is what looks like a paper-knife still in the wound, which I wouldn't mind betting did not come from the rather fancy Victorian bureau set on the desk next to the body."

Constable raised an eyebrow. "Doing our job for us now, doc?"

The doctor gave a cross between a snort and a smile. "Just being observant. It's modern, unlike the desk set, which is all there anyway, as far as I can see. And a bit late for a change of career on my part, Andy, wouldn't you say? I just happened to notice, that's all. Anyway, there's the bones of it. Nothing more I can do here, so if it's all right by you, I'll be off, and I'll get some transport organised to take the lady away for me to have a closer look at, back in the lab. Not that I'm anticipating any surprises."

"I bet you're in for one surprise at least, doctor," said Copper. "They're bound to have a farewell party organised back at the station. You won't want to miss out on that."

"They'd better not," retorted the doctor. "No fuss, that's what I said. I'm planning on sidling away quietly. And if you'll take my advice, Andy, you'll do the same when your time comes. Meanwhile, I'll leave things in the hands of you members of the younger generation."

Constable gave a chuckle. "Not so young any more, doc," he said ruefully. "Every time I look in the mirror I see a few more grey hairs." He extended a hand. "Anyway, thanks for everything. It's been a pleasure."

"Me too, doc." Copper shook the older man's hand.

"By the way, doc," added Constable, "I probably don't need to invoke patient confidentiality, but I'm under orders to stop any word of this getting out for now ..."

"... and you'd prefer it if I didn't go broadcasting what's happened here? Understood. My minions will be appropriately instructed." A dry smile. "I've been exercising discretion for so many years, sometimes I don't even tell myself what I'm up to." Without another word, the doctor turned and made his way out of the front door.

Sheila Deare, who had faded into the background when the doctor appeared, stepped forward. "I expect you still want to see the body, Andy, now that you know what the doctor's had to say."

"Of course," said Constable, his hand on the door-knob.

"And then interview everyone else in the house in turn?"

"It seems sensible. Probably starting with

the one who first found the body."

"Which was Philip Knightly."

"The hotel manager, I think you said?"

"That's right. He's in his office, which is what used to be the old butler's pantry."

"I know it. Just here off the hall."

"So if you like, I can tell him to expect you shortly, and then I'd better go tell the ministers what's going on, and that you'll be up to see them in a little while." Sheila sighed. "That's probably going to take a great deal of time and tact. I'm expecting quite a lot of ruffled feathers. Especially from Mrs. Nye. She'll probably want to muscle in and take over, being Justice Secretary. It won't be easy telling her she's been outranked by the Deputy P.M."

"You have my sympathy," said Constable. "No doubt I shall come in for my fair share of problems when I speak to everyone, being a mere humble detective inspector. But yes, do by all means go and attend to all that, and Copper and I will make a start by taking a look at your late boss." He opened the library door.

Chapter 2

"Well, at least we've got the means, guv," said Dave Copper, looking down once again at the body. "The doc was pretty clear on that, so you haven't got to unravel some sort of unholy tangle like with that business in the horse-racing case. Just the motive and opportunity to go."

"With a group of politicians," replied Andy Constable. "Well, I can't imagine that any of them would have anything to hide." A wry look. "We are going to have to tread very carefully."

"Behind you all the way, guv," said Copper, unable to suppress a grin. "It's probably the safest place to be. So, my notebook is standing by. You wanted to talk to this manager chap, didn't you? So shall we?"

Constable gave a wry smile. "Taking charge, eh? Getting in some practice to be investigating officer?"

"Not just yet, sir. Not just yet."

"And you know where to find this Mr. Knightly?"

"Inspector Deare said he was in the old butler's pantry. Which is through that little hidden door under the stairs, sir, isn't it?"

"Your powers of recall are astounding, sergeant," said Constable admiringly. "Well, you'd better lead the way."

The door to the former butler's pantry was, as Dave Copper remembered, almost perfectly concealed in the wood panelling of the staircase.

Inside, in contrast to the shadowy and atmospheric ambience of the main hall, the bright spot-lighting came almost as a shock, reflected as it was off the surfaces of chrome, glass and gleaming laminate which featured in the room's modernist furnishings. Metal filing cabinets were lined up against one white-painted wall, a combined desk and computer work station in pale Scandinavian wood stood against another. And seated at the desk, gazing unfocussed at the blank computer screen, sat a man. Somewhere in his forties, Constable estimated, with dark hair cut in extremely fashionable modern style and a face which, but for its present careworn expression, would probably have exuded smiling enthusiasm. He looked up, startled, as the police officers entered the room.

"Mr. Knightly?"

"Yes," replied the man in slightly uncertain tones. He stood. "What do you want?"

"Detective Inspector Constable, sir." Constable showed his warrant card. "This is my colleague Detective Sergeant Copper. And I'm sure you can guess why we're here."

"Yes. Inspector Deare said you'd be in." A deep sigh. "You'd better sit down." The man gestured to two uncomfortable-looking upright steel seats, and then slumped back into his white leather swivel armchair. "God, this is awful." He rested his elbows on his desk and put his head in his hands.

"I can quite understand your feelings, sir,"

said Constable. "It must have been a shock. I'm told you were the one who discovered the body of the Prime Minister. Which means, I'm afraid, that we have to ask you some questions."

"Of course, inspector. What would you like to know?"

"I think we'd better start with the basics, sir. Your name."

"Philip Knightly. That's with one 'l', sergeant," said the man, observing Copper beginning to make notes. "But 'Phil' will do."

"And you are the manager of the hotel?" resumed Constable.

"Yes. I was the one responsible for setting the place up when the company bought the Hall, and I've been running it ever since."

"Very much a full-time job, I imagine, sir. That must be very demanding. No time at all for breaks?"

"Scarcely, inspector," smiled Phil wanly. "It comes with the territory. Although I did actually manage to take a whole weekend off last year. Around this time, as it happens. The directors took pity on me, because it was my birthday."

"Made one or two changes, I notice," remarked Constable, looking around the room. "The sergeant and I had occasion to come here some while ago on a previous case," he explained in response to the manager's puzzled look. "This was the old butler's pantry then, although they were using it as some sort of drinks store."

"Oh, we still do," said Phil. "Well, the old strongroom in that corner is used to keep our fine wines in. Some of them can come out at over a thousand pounds a bottle, so you want to keep them somewhere secure. But as for this room, I needed an office close to the action, and I didn't want to take up one of the good rooms of the house – the company likes to keep the hotels as much as possible as they were when they were private houses – so I tuck myself away in here."

"Very modern, sir." Constable nodded approvingly.

"We've redecorated and modernised the bedrooms too. Made them all en-suite. But the rooms down here are probably pretty much as you'll remember them, if you've been here before. So how did that come about?"

"Another murder, sir, as it happens."

"What?"

"You didn't know, sir?"

Philip looked shocked. "I had no idea."

"Probably not the sort of thing the former owners would be too anxious to publicise, guv," put in Dave Copper. "Might have dented the asking price a bit. And even if the new owners did know about the murder at the fête, they probably wouldn't want the fact too widely known. Might put people off coming to stay here."

"Even so, I'm surprised, Mr. Knightly," said Constable. "I wouldn't have thought it was possible to keep something like that from getting out. Village gossip, and all. Of course, there may have been a touch of local loyalty to it – you know, respect for the people up at the big house.

Not that any of this is relevant to anything, as far as I can see. We have a completely new case on our hands."

"Other than the fact that nobody wants anything about this one to get out, guv," put in Copper.

"Yes, thank you, sergeant," responded Constable with a touch of asperity. "I'm assuming that fact has already been made quite clear to Mr. Knightly."

"Yes. Inspector Deare said that I wasn't to say a word to anyone."

"Which of course excludes us, sir. So, if you can cast your mind back to this morning, can you tell us exactly what happened."

Phil gave a slightly helpless shrug. "There isn't really that much to tell. I got up this morning about half past six as usual ..."

"You live on the premises, sir?" interrupted Copper.

"Yes. I've got a small flat in the old servants rooms up in the attics."

"Just you, sir? Nobody else lives in?"

"Normally, yes, they do. The chef and the housekeeper have got rooms up there as well, but I was told to give them a few extra days paid leave at the government's expense, so they went off quite happily yesterday morning."

"Were they told what was due to take place here?"

"No," replied Phil. "I was ordered to keep everything completely secret. They'll be back on Monday." A grimace. "They'll get a bit of a shock when they find out what's happened."

"And just to clarify, sir, what about other staff?"

"The cleaners and waiting staff and so on all come up from the village. But they're all off until Monday too."

"Which is why, presumably, it was necessary to bring in one of the catering staff from Number 10," said Constable. "Well, we shall be speaking to him in due course. But for now, let's carry on with what happened this morning."

"Well, as I say, I got up, had my shower, and came down for seven o'clock as usual to get the breakfast ready."

"Is that normally your job, Mr. Knightly?"

"Not normally, inspector. That's usually the chef's province, of course. I can if I need to. It was all part of my degree in hotel management. But the orders were that breakfast was mostly going to be a continental cold buffet, with the majority of the stuff brought in from Downing Street. But I would have got the dining room ready with Jim – that's the chap from number 10 – and then just overseen everything while he got on with things in the kitchen."

"So, you came down ..." prompted Constable.

"Yes. I came down the servants' stairs into the kitchen ..."

"I remember those from when we were here before, guv," put in Dave Copper. "You don't get many houses with secret passages and whatnot. Not that they had anything to do with the case, but I remember being quite tickled at the time."

"Actually, you're not the only one, sergeant," said Phil. "Some of our guests are rather intrigued by them, especially the Americans. They start asking silly questions about priest's holes and treasure, and I'm afraid some of the staff do lead them on rather, showing them the hidden doors and making up a few stories. I don't encourage it, but it's all quite harmless."

"And totally irrelevant to this investigation, sergeant," said Constable severely. "We'll stick to the point, if you don't mind. So, Mr. Knightly, you were saying. You came downstairs ..."

"Yes, inspector. Sorry. Well, I put the water heater on for the tea and coffee, and then, as Inspector Deare and Jim hadn't arrived, I thought I'd have a quick check around the rooms to make sure they were in good order – see that nobody had left any wet glasses leaving sticky rings on the tables last night, that sort of thing – so I went around the rooms in turn. Dining room, drawing room, morning room, and lastly into the library." Phil stopped short at the recollection.

"And ...?"

"And there she was. Mrs. Ronson. Lying there, face down, with the knife in her back." A pause. "My knife."

Constable sat up in surprise. "Yours, sir?"

"Yes." Phil gestured. "It lives here, on my desk. It's silver – Swedish – it was a present from my parents when I got my degree. I recognised it straight away."

"So what then, Mr. Knightly?"

"I didn't know what to do. I didn't like to touch her, but I could see she wasn't breathing. And then I came out into the hall, and I could see Inspector Deare and Jim just arriving at the front door, so I went to unlock it to let them in, told them what I'd found, and the inspector took charge straight away."

"So the front door had been locked up until this time?"

"Yes. All the doors were. Inspector Deare insisted, seeing that she wasn't going to be on the premises after she left yesterday evening."

"And how many keys are there?"

"Just two master sets. I keep one, and the other is usually in my safe, but I'd let Inspector Deare have it last night, just in case. And all the external doors are alarmed anyway. I mean, you can get out in an emergency."

"But nobody could have entered or left the premises without your knowledge between the time that the ministers returned last night and the time you came down this morning?"

"No, inspector."

Constable thought for a moment. "Hmmm. I'm wondering if that's going to make our job harder or easier," he remarked in an aside to Copper. "So, just to rewind for a moment, Mr. Knightly, let's go back to yesterday. I take it you knew who was coming."

"Of course. I'd had to allocate the rooms."

"And the ministers all arrived more or less

together around tea-time yesterday, I think. Tell me, had you met any of them beforehand?"

"Met them? No. Well ... Not really. I mean I'd seen them all on the news at various times, so I knew who they were."

Constable frowned. "I may be mistaken, but you seemed a little unsure for a moment. Sir?"

"Well ... I don't actually know any of them. It's just that I recognised one of them from my college."

"Oh yes, sir?"

"Yes. Mr. Grade."

"The Education Secretary?"

"Yes. I mean, I didn't really know him," Phil explained hastily. "We weren't friends or anything like that. We were a couple of years apart, and anyway, he was on a different course. Engineering, or some such – well, something mechanical, I think. One of those things involving metalwork, anyway. Being on the hospitality course, we didn't really mix with people from that side of things. We were the Foodies, and we called them the Spannermen. But it's years ago. I almost didn't recognise him, and I doubt if he'd remember me."

"Did you mention this to anyone? Mrs. Ronson, perhaps?"

"Only in passing. Talk of funny coincidences – that sort of thing."

"But you knew none of the others? You're quite sure, sir?" pressed Constable.

"Positive."

"So, after everybody arrived ...?"

"People went up to their rooms for a little while to unpack and settle in, and then they came back down to the drawing room for drinks. We've got a small bar set up in a corner. The Prime Minister gave a short speech – well, it was more of an announcement, really. She said that despite the fact that the government had only been in for a short time, she felt for various reasons that it was time to consider a cabinet reshuffle. She said that one of the most interesting things about being P.M. was the fact that you were constantly making new discoveries. I'm not sure anybody quite understood – there was a lot of exchanging of looks. And then people broke up into twos and threes in there and in the morning room, and I got on with serving the drinks."

"I don't suppose," hazarded Constable, "you would have heard anything while you were doing so which might have had a bearing on what happened later?"

"You mean, did I hear anybody threatening to kill Mrs. Ronson?" said Phil in disbelieving tones.

"I think you'd probably have volunteered that fact by now, Mr. Knightly," replied Constable with a grim smile.

"The only person I heard Mrs. Ronson speak to was Miss Laye."

Constable wrinkled his brow for a moment.

"Foreign Secretary, guv," prompted Copper helpfully.

"Thank you, sergeant."

"And as far as I could hear," went on Phil, "the conversation was completely innocent. Mrs. Ronson said that she wanted to hear all about Mrs. Laye's trip, because she'd just got back from an overseas visit, so they'd need to have a quiet talk later, but now wasn't the time. The P.M. said something about taking a great interest in foreign affairs because they could sometimes be very dangerous. Something of a minefield, she said. And there was some mention of the Gulf. But that was about as threatening as it got."

"Anyone else?"

"I don't think so. Oh ... wait a minute. I went into the morning room, and Deborah Nye and Marion Hayste were talking in a corner. They didn't actually notice me when I went in, because there's a screen by the door to stop any draughts. But Mrs. Hayste was saying something about needing a boost, and Mrs. Nye made some remark about 'that's what all your prison inmates would say, wouldn't they?', and the regime would have to change right now or there'd be trouble. Someone would have to pay, and not just the usual people. I thought, I don't think I'm supposed to be hearing rows about government policy, so I gave my best manager's cough and asked them if I could get them anything to drink. And Mrs. Nye snapped 'That's the last thing she needs right now', so I just turned round and got out double quick."

"And that was it? Nothing else from anyone else?"

"Pretty much," said Phil after a moment's

consideration. "A few remarks about the weather. What the view was like from people's rooms. That sort of thing. But it wasn't too long before they all got organised to go off down to the village inn for dinner, and they came back a couple of hours later."

"And then?"

"Well, at that point, Mrs. Ronson said that nobody else from the staff would be needed, so she sent Inspector Deare off. I gathered that the plan was for the Prime Minister to have individual talks with the ministers, so I suggested that she'd probably like to use the library, and I said that I'd leave the bar open in the drawing room for anyone who wanted to use it. Then I took myself off up to my flat and settled down with a couple of glasses of wine and a video. And I went to bed about half past eleven, I suppose."

"And you heard nothing to give you any concern during that time?"

"I'm up in the eaves, inspector. You could fire a gun down here and I probably wouldn't hear it." Phil stopped short and closed his eyes. "Sorry, inspector. That was a pretty stupid thing to say."

"Don't let it worry you, sir. Thankfully, nobody's been firing any guns. Your knife seems to have been quite sufficient to commit the crime. And I imagine that we shall find your fingerprints all over it. Which may not look too good for you."

"But I didn't ...," spluttered Phil. "I mean, I

wouldn't ... I'd have no reason ..."

"Calm down, sir," interrupted Constable. "That wasn't an accusation. Merely an observation. But for now, that would seem to bring us full circle, so we'll leave it there for the moment. I'd be obliged if you'd stay put and not communicate with anyone else for the time being." The inspector stood, and made his way back out into the hall, Copper in his wake. A thought struck him, and he turned to his junior colleague. "Copper, get on your phone to your friend Sergeant Singleton at SOCO. She is back on our turf from Westchester, isn't she?"

"Una, sir? But Inspector Deare said ..."

"I don't care what she said. This is my investigation, and if I have to ignore one or two orders, I shall do so. But discreetly. So get on the phone to Singleton and get her up here. In civvies, and not a word to a soul. I don't want speculation running round the station."

"Shouldn't be a problem, guv. It's her day off anyway. But she'll be at home. So I'll just ..." Copper broke off, blushing.

Constable smiled slowly. "Is there by any chance something you've been forgetting to tell me about your domestic arrangements? Well, no matter now. But get on to that, and then prime Sergeant Collins at the gate to let her through. Oh, and you'd better tell him to expect a nice anonymous black van to collect the victim, if the doc hasn't already done so."

"Righty-ho, guv." Copper turned away and began to murmur into his phone.

As Copper was speaking, the sound of footsteps was heard above the detectives, and Sheila Deare appeared as she descended the stairs. She looked worn.

"All well?" enquired Constable.

"I wouldn't go so far as to say that," replied Sheila with a wan smile. "But I've explained to everyone what's happened – just the bare bones – and I've told them to expect you shortly. I'm afraid they're getting a bit restive – not having had any breakfast, the pangs of hunger are starting to kick in. Is there any chance of at least sorting out that problem?"

"Ignoring the political and international implications of what we're facing? Why not? They say the longest journey begins with a single step," responded Constable with a wry laugh. He thought for a moment. "Well, I'm not having anyone wandering about the house ad lib until I've had a chance to talk to them. I don't want any cross-contamination or collusion. So, as Mr. Knightly was supposed to be organising breakfast, why don't we get him to do just that? Tell him to get himself into the kitchen and put up something on a tray for everyone, and then he can take it up to their rooms. And no chat – just in and out. That'll give him something to occupy himself while Copper and I are doing the rounds."

"Don't forget, guv, Inspector Deare said that waiter chap is in the kitchen," intervened Copper. "If you don't want anyone talking to anyone ..."

Constable sighed. "Good grief. This is like a

game of chess. Right. Is there anyone in the morning room?" Sheila shook her head. "Good. Put the waiter in there, and we'll speak to him once we've faced these various lions in their dens. Do you want to come and sit in on that, Sheila?"

"Best not," she replied. "I don't think I'm especially popular upstairs at the moment, and I don't want to distract from your enquiries. Besides, I have things to do. I've got to keep the Deputy P.M. up to date with what's going on. That's my main job at the moment. Although whether I'll still be in post at the end of the day is anybody's guess. Careers like mine probably don't survive events like this."

Constable nodded in sympathy. "Well, we'll leave you to your duties, and we'll get on with ours. Notebook at the ready, Copper – I have a suspicion you may be about to take copious notes." He set his foot on the first tread of the stairs.

Chapter 3

"So where do we start, guv?" asked Dave Copper.

"Excellent question, sergeant," said Andy Constable, standing at the head of the stairs. "To which the only answer is, I have no idea. I don't suppose Mr. Knightly mentioned which rooms these people are in?"

"Sorry, guv, no. I've just got the names."

"Then we shall start at the end and work round. Let's go along here to the left. I think that was the room we saw the vicar in before, if I'm not much mistaken."

"That's right, sir. Full of Chinese furniture wasn't it?"

"I think it was. That's probably where they've put the Foreign Secretary. Well, let's find out."

A tap at the door, which bore a small decorative ceramic plate with the words 'Chinese Bedroom' in confirmation of Copper's recollection, produced no reply.

"Maybe they're in the bathroom, sir."

After a further fruitless knock, Constable opened the door with a tentative 'Hello?' There was no response. He advanced into the darkened room and with a loud 'Ow!', barked his shins on a low table in front of the fireplace. "Copper, get those curtains open," he ordered in irritated tones, and the sergeant hastened to obey.

"So whose room is this, guv?" wondered

Copper. "And if everyone's been told to stay put, where are they?"

"I think we have our answer to that, sergeant," said Constable. He pointed to a large briefcase lying open on the foot of the bed. Square and sturdy, it was covered in bright red tooled leather and bore, in embossed gold lettering, the simple legend 'Prime Minister'. "As to the occupant, we know exactly where she is. Lying on the library floor. And the fact that the curtains were closed, and the bed hasn't been slept in, tells us something else. We can now make a pretty good guess as to when Mrs. Ronson was killed. It was obviously some time last night rather than this morning, which ties in with the doctor's comments."

"Do you want to check the room out, as we're here? There may be something helpful lying about," suggested Copper hopefully.

"I think on balance not. I get the impression from Inspector Deare that we've got a bunch of politicians hopping about like cats on hot bricks, and I'd rather not have them any more unhappy than they already are. So we'll come back here once we've done the circuit." Constable turned and made his way back out into the corridor, knocked on the next door whose plate read 'Blue Bedroom', and, in response to the brisk 'Yes?' from within, entered.

The room did not belie its name. The carpet and the profusion of cushions scattered on the bed provided a palette of pale blue shades and patterns, while the mantelpiece bore several statement pieces of classic Wedgwood china. At the window were swagged blue curtains featuring a design of eighteenth-century Arcadian scenes. And beneath them, in a regency armchair, sat a woman. She looked to be in her fifties, slim, with chin-length iron-grey hair swept to one side across her brow, and piercing grey eyes. Her jacket and skirt were severe, black with touches of white trim. She rose to her feet with an enquiring look.

"Good morning, madam," began Constable. "My name is Detective Inspector Constable – this is my colleague Detective Sergeant Copper." The two proffered their warrant cards. "I wonder if we might have a few minutes of your time?"

"I hope, inspector, before we go any further, that you'll provide some sort of explanation of this extraordinary situation I find myself in," was the frosty reply. "I am not accustomed to being held in virtual solitary confinement, and I'm not at all sure as to the authority under which these measures are being taken."

"My apologies, madam." Constable's tones were at their most emollient. "But we are all acting under orders which have come from the most senior authority, namely the Deputy Prime Minister. I believe Inspector Deare will have told you what has occurred."

"That the Prime Minister is dead? Yes."

"Not just dead, madam. Murdered."

"You're certain? There's no possible doubt?" was the sharp response.

"None whatever," said Constable. "I have seen the body, as has our police doctor. There is no other explanation. And so I have to ask some questions of those people who were in this house at the relevant time."

"You believe that this was done by one of the people in the house last night? One of my colleagues?" The disbelief was plain to hear in the minister's voice.

"I'm afraid that the evidence is pointing in that direction, madam."

"Hmmm. I shall be interested to hear your evidence, inspector. We'll see how it might play in court."

"I'm sorry?"

"I used to be a barrister before I came into this business of politics, inspector." A dry smile. "That was when the criminals were neatly on the other side of the bar. And now you seem to be telling me that I've fallen into their company."

Constable cleared his throat. "I think we may be getting a little ahead of ourselves. At the moment I'm more anxious to establish details of the people and the events of yesterday which led up to the killing of Mrs. Ronson. So if we may start with some of the basics ..."

"Of course." The woman subsided into her chair and waved towards a small matching sofa at the foot of the bed, on to which the detectives squeezed with some difficulty.

"My sergeant will take notes, if you have no objection," said Constable. "So for his benefit, if you could give your name."

The woman raised her eyebrows slightly. "Deborah Nye," she replied. "Mrs., if you need to know. And also for your benefit, sergeant, you might like to note that I am Secretary of State for Justice, and Lord Chancellor."

"Thank you, Mrs. Nye. I suppose that makes you my boss," ventured Copper with a tentative smile.

"No. That pleasure falls to the Home Secretary."

"Oh. Sorry for the interruption." In response to a sideways look from his superior, Copper buried his nose in his notebook.

"And you are all here for this meeting at the instigation of the late Prime Minister, I gather," resumed Constable. "Would you have any insight as to how this came about?"

"None in particular," said Deborah. "There were some mutterings beforehand that she might be considering a re-shuffle, which all seemed rather premature as we haven't really been in office that long. But the official word was that she wanted to have private conversations with each of us – I assumed that it would all be with a view to finding out how each of us was settling into our portfolios and whether we had any insights yet as to how things might be improved."

"But yet, as I understand it, only some of the Cabinet were involved. Not the whole group." Constable essayed a small smile. "Not, for instance, Copper's boss the Home Secretary."

"Who is off in the United States delivering a

speech on border security. It's the sort of thing that happens at a time like this when Parliament isn't sitting. We tend to take the opportunity to carry out some overseas trips, like the one Mandy's just come back from."

"Mandy?"

"Sorry. Amanda Laye, the Foreign Secretary."

"We've not met her yet."

"She spends half her life on the road, it seems to me. Or in the air. However, she's here, as am I, and we seem to be diverging from the point somewhat."

"Which was your conversation with the Prime Minister, I think. And had that already taken place?"

"We'd talked, yes. Of course, there was general conversation as people were arriving, and then there was some sort of get-together for drinks before we went off for dinner, but it wasn't until after we'd come back from the village that Doris started calling people in for their private chats in the library. I suppose that must have been some time after nine o'clock."

"Of course, during this 'get-together' you mention, you'd already had some sort of a 'private chat', as you put it, with one of your colleagues, hadn't you?" said Constable smoothly. "Only the manager Mr. Knightly mentioned something. With Mrs. Hayste, I think, wasn't it?"

"Marion?" Deborah seemed slightly disconcerted. "Oh yes, that. Marion and the drugs business." The minister stopped short. "Sorry, inspector – please forget I said that. It's ... it's a policy matter. I shouldn't have spoken of it. It was just a thought that popped up regarding part of her responsibilities. She's my Number Two in my Department, of course, so there's always something. In fact, we'd come down together in my car."

"Plenty of time there for a little chat, I would have thought," murmured Constable, but then continued swiftly before the minister could react. "So, re-capping, you arrived, had drinks, went to the Dammett Well Inn for a private dinner, and went to talk with the Prime Minister after you returned. Do you by any chance remember what sequence people were seen?"

"I'm not really sure. I know Mandy was first in, and then it was Lew. That's Lewis Stalker, the Culture Secretary," she added in response to Copper's querying look. "I was third, and then Milo Grade was after me. After that, I'm afraid I really can't tell you, because I then came up to my room because I wanted to read. There's a limit to the amount of time one can tolerate one's colleagues in what is supposed to pass as a social situation." A bleak smile.

"And did you leave this room after that?" asked the inspector.

"No. I still haven't. Which is why you must forgive me, Mr. Constable, if I reacted a little like a caged tiger when you first arrived."

"Can you tell me anything about your conversation with Mrs. Ronson? Or between her and any of your colleagues?" Constable did not hold out much hope of an informative answer. He was to be proved correct.

"I'm afraid I have to invoke cabinet confidentiality, inspector. I really can't be expected to reveal anything concerning what was discussed, and of course I would have no idea what was said between the Prime Minister and the others."

"She didn't, for example, mention why this particular group was called together rather than any of your other ministerial colleagues?"

"She did not."

"So you would have no inkling why anyone from the party might wish to kill her?"

"No, inspector." Deborah looked Constable straight in the eye. "Not the slightest idea."

*

"That was helpful, guv," murmured Dave Copper in discreetly lowered tones as the two detectives found themselves back in the corridor. "Three wise monkeys rolled into one – saw no evil, heard no evil, spoke no evil."

"Not the first time we've ever encountered that situation," replied Andy Constable. "But, early days. Let's see if we can crowbar any more out of the others. Starting with the occupant of the ..." He consulted the plaque on the bedroom door. "... the Yellow Bedroom."

After a cheery 'Come in!' from within the room, the detectives entered to find the occupant seated propped up on the bed, busily demolishing a marmalade-laden croissant. In his forties, with a stocky frame, dark hair and eyes, and a blunt nose, he wore jeans and an open-necked shirt above bare feet.

"Sorry to interrupt you, sir." Constable performed the introductions. "But you'll be aware of the situation, so we are beginning to make enquiries."

"Of course. Go right ahead. Only you won't mind if I carry on having breakfast, will you? I'm absolutely starving, not having had a thing since last night. Take a seat." The man waved to a pair of tub chairs flanking the fireplace. "Would you like some coffee? I'm sure there's plenty, if you can find some cups."

"We won't, thank you, sir," declined Constable. "We have a number of people to see, so we'd best begin. My colleague here will note down some details."

"Okay, fine. Right – name, rank, and serial number, I suppose? Milo Grade. I'm the Secretary of State for Education, and as for serial number, please don't ask me where I fit into the cabinet hierarchy because I haven't the faintest idea. Somewhere undistinguished in the middle, I dare say." He dunked his croissant into his coffee cup. "God, that's a life-saver. Thank goodness that chap brought the tray up just now."

"Oh, Mr. Knightly, the manager? Yes, we asked him to arrange some breakfasts. But … forgive me, but I got the impression that you knew him already."

"Him?" Milo furrowed his brow. "No, I don't think so. Where from?"

"He mentioned something about you having been to the same educational establishment as him."

Milo shrugged. "Sorry. Means nothing. I probably don't have to tell you how many people are undergoing education in this country at any one time." A grin. "Actually, I probably couldn't tell you. But that's what civil servants are for, isn't it?" He grew serious. "But that's not what you're here about, is it? You'll have to forgive me. I tend to get flippant when I'm nervous."

"You're nervous, sir?"

"Who wouldn't be? The Prime Minister gets killed, and after what happened yesterday you're bound to be looking at people in something of a suspicious light."

"After what happened yesterday, sir?" echoed Constable, his attention sharpened. "So you think that yesterday's events have a direct bearing on Mrs. Ronson's death? I don't suppose you'd care to be a little more specific?"

Milo wriggled slightly. "I don't think I would, inspector," he said evasively. "What I mean is, with the P.M. having private conversations with everybody, and there being talk of a re-shuffle in the air, I think everyone was justified in looking a bit nervous last night."

"Including yourself, sir?"

"Doubly so now." Milo attempted a smile, which did not wholly convince. "There'll be a new P.M. with their own ideas as to who should be doing what. It's a rough old game, politics. But nobody goes into it with the intention of getting the sack."

"And how did you get into it, sir, just as a matter of interest?" Constable's enquiry sounded blandly conversational.

"Oh, the usual route," replied Milo. "Studied PPE – that's Politics, Philosophy and Economics if you want the whole mouthful, sergeant," he added in response to Copper's frown. "Got a First, actually. And then I applied for a job as a research assistant to an M.P., and when I told them about the degree, they gave it to me straight off. After that I eventually got offered a parliamentary seat, which I won first go. In fact, I'm probably one of those politicians people talk about who've never had a proper job." He gave a slightly uneasy laugh.

"So although you're in charge of education, you've never been a teacher? Mightn't that be a little awkward sometimes, sir?"

"Well, you know what they say, inspector – those who can, do, and those who can't, teach. But I think it's better to tell the teachers what to do."

"Which, I assume, is why Mrs. Ronson put you into your post, sir. So, let's come back to the events of yesterday. Now, we've been told that most people arrived here at the Hall at more or less the same time late yesterday afternoon, and then there was something of an informal gathering before you all left to have the private dinner at the inn in Dammett Worthy. And then everyone returned here and a series of meetings began. May I take it that all this applies to yourself?"

"That's pretty much it, inspector."

"Can you think of anything that occurred that might have a bearing on the case, sir? Any noticeable tensions between Mrs. Ronson and any of your colleagues? Any overt hostility? Anything that anyone might have let slip?"

Milo considered for a few seconds. "Nothing that I can put my finger on. We're politicians, inspector – we're used to keeping our cards pretty close to our chests." He stopped abruptly. "Oh."

"You've thought of something, sir?"

"I don't suppose it means anything."

"Well, let's hear it anyway, sir," encouraged Constable.

"I was in the back of the P.M.'s car with her and Benny – sorry, sergeant, that's the Social Security Secretary, Benjamin Fitt. I can see that you're scribbling frantically, trying to keep up with me."

"I'm doing fine, sir," said Copper, whose expression belied his words. "You carry on."

"Okay. Anyway, we were on our way down to the village, and she leant across to Benny and said something about wanting to have a good long talk about family policy. She said there were some specifics she wanted to sort out. I wouldn't normally eavesdrop, but I think she was trying to keep her voice down, and it's only natural human curiosity to earwig, isn't it? And he muttered something which I didn't catch, and she said something like 'It's dealing with close family relationships that I'm most bothered about. And we all have to be completely above reproach in everything we do, don't we?'"

"Did you get any inkling of what they were referring to?"

"Not my department, inspector. I've got quite enough to do without worrying about policy decisions in somebody else's ministry. And anyway, we were just arriving at the village pub, so we all got out, and that was the end of that. And of course, there was a total ban on shop talk over dinner."

"But you yourself had talks with the Prime Minister when you returned here later. Which I dare say you aren't prepared to discuss with me."

"Got it in one, I'm afraid, inspector."

"Can you offhand recall the order of these discussions, sir? You never know, it may be relevant."

"Some of them, certainly. I know Mandy and Lew were early on, and then Dee was before me, and I was asked to send Erica Mayall after me. I didn't really notice what happened after that – I just had a couple more drinks and a bit of a chat with Perry, and then went off to bed, where I slept the sleep of the just until Inspector Deare came knocking this morning."

"You saw and heard nothing further? You weren't about the house at any point after that?"

"Sorry, inspector." A bland smile. "Can't help you."

Chapter 4

"I don't know about you, guv, but I got next to nothing out of that," commented Dave Copper as the bedroom door closed behind the pair. "Except maybe a touch of writer's cramp."

"You may be in for rather more of that by the time we've finished, sergeant," answered Andy Constable. "As for your other point, I'm not so sure. Those two have both been pretty tight-lipped over the whole situation, but I've noticed one or two little moments that made me wonder what's bubbling under the surface. I'm sure there's something."

"Other than the fact that it looks as if people were jumpy about losing their jobs? You can understand that, can't you?"

"Ah, but why?" Constable squared his shoulders. "Well, let's carry on trying to find out." He examined the plaque on the next door. "'Her Ladyship's Room', eh? This sounds extremely grand. I wonder which of our band of politicos qualified for that honour." He tapped at the door.

"Yes?" The door was thrown open almost immediately by a mature woman wearing an emerald green two-piece suit of evidently, even to Constable's untutored eye, designer origin. Her dark blonde hair fell to her shoulders in soft waves, and her grey eyes, even shielded by the severe heavy-framed glasses she wore, were piercing. She was tall, almost tall enough to look Constable straight in the eye. Her tone changed to one of disappointment. "Oh."

"I hope this isn't a bad moment, madam." The inspector offered his identification. Copper followed suit. "I wonder if we might come in."

The woman held back the door wordlessly and gestured the detectives into the room. "Sit," she ordered brusquely, but continued to pace restlessly in front of the fireplace as Constable and Copper took seats on a chaise longue at the foot of the curtained four-poster bed.

"You are of course aware of the situation, I'm sure," began Constable. "I imagine Inspector Deare will have filled you in on the basic facts."

"She has. She has also taken it under her own authority to place me, and I assume all my colleagues, under what I can only describe as a form of house arrest. Which I am certain exceeds her remit. I shall be asking some very pertinent questions when all this is over."

"I believe her authority comes from the very top, madam," pointed out Constable in an attempt to calm the obviously irritated minister. "She is simply following her orders. As am I, which means that I need to ask you some questions about the events of the past twenty-four hours."

The woman consulted her watch. "Or in my case, inspector, eighteen hours, since my plane didn't touch down until yesterday afternoon. I hope you won't be expecting me to account for my movements at thirty-five thousand feet."

"Of course not, madam." A small smile. "Which leads me to suppose that you would be the Foreign Secretary." The woman raised her eyebrows. "Forgive me, but the demands of my job don't leave me much time to keep up with the minutiae of politics or foreign affairs."

A self-deprecating half-laugh. The woman's mood became markedly less confrontational. "Thank you for the small and timely reality check, inspector. I'm afraid that those of us who live in ivory towers among the international great and good tend to forget that, to most ordinary people, we're supremely unimportant. So yes, your assumption is correct – I'm Amanda Laye, Her Majesty's Principal Secretary of State for Foreign and Commonwealth Affairs." Copper's pen hovered uncertainly. "Sergeant, feel free to abbreviate that to 'Foreign Secretary'."

"Is that 'Mrs' Laye, madam?" queried Copper.

"Miss."

"Thank you."

"So, Miss Laye," resumed Constable, "I gather you arrived here quite late yesterday."

"Not especially," countered Amanda. "Although I was probably the last one to get here, because my flight only arrived in the afternoon."

"I only ask because somebody heard the Prime Minister mention that she wanted to have a talk with you about foreign affairs, but there wasn't time then."

"That would probably be because all the private meetings were scheduled for later," said Amanda smoothly. She subsided elegantly on to an armchair alongside Constable. "These things never go well when they're rushed."

"But, of course, you might have had a chance to cover things briefly during your journey down to the village for dinner."

"Oh no, inspector. The P.M. and I were in separate cars. I went down in Inspector Deare's car with Erica, Lew, Dee and Perry."

"Although, of course, this whole gathering wouldn't primarily have been about this latest trip of yours," surmised Constable. "Otherwise your colleagues wouldn't all have been called together. So what, do you suppose, might have been the reason?"

Amanda shrugged. "I really couldn't say, inspector. The P.M. was very reticent about the motivation behind the whole thing. I think we probably all thought we were being sized up for new jobs in an impending re-shuffle."

"Be that as it may, you were I think the first to have a meeting with the Prime Minister when the party returned here from the village after dinner." A look towards Copper. "Sergeant, correct me if I'm wrong?"

A riffle back through the pages of Copper's notebook. "That's what we were told, sir."

"Any special reason, do you suppose, Miss Laye? Other than, obviously, the seniority of your position?"

"Not particularly, inspector. You appreciate, of course, that I couldn't divulge any details of confidential discussions."

Constable sighed inwardly. "No, of course, Miss Laye. I'm coming to realise that. So I'll have to assume that it was simply the first opportunity to review the future and to catch up on the details of your recent travels. I think someone heard Mrs. Ronson mention an interest in affairs in the Gulf."

There was a tiny hesitation before Amanda replied. "But I hadn't been to the Gulf, inspector. This trip was to the Far East – Singapore and Malaysia."

"How odd. I dare say the remark was misheard."

Another pause, and then the frown on Amanda's face cleared. "Of course – I remember there was talk of the gulf between expectations and reality, inspector." She gave a slightly brittle half-laugh. "That's what it must have been."

Quietly resolving to give the matter more thought later, Constable chose to move on. "And after your meeting with Mrs. Ronson, what did you do?"

"I stayed around downstairs for a little while. I helped myself to a drink, and then I found myself next to Erica Mayall so I settled down for a chat with her. We swapped a few traveller's tales – her job takes her away to some extent, looking into the situation of women's rights in various countries, but we were mostly talking about our favourite shops and restaurants around the world. It was entirely frivolous – nothing to do with work at all. But we ran out of conversation after a while – it's not as if we're particularly close friends. And eventually the atmosphere began to feel like one of those waiting rooms where people are lined up for interviews, and then they disappear one by one as the tension mounts, so I decided to come back up here and put my feet up with a book."

"Which would have been at what time?"

Amanda pondered. "Some time after ten, I suppose, but I couldn't be any more accurate than that."

"Did you leave your room after that? Or were you aware of anyone else doing so?"

"You mean, was there any of the classic country house situation we've all seen in the Sunday night dramas, with people furtively creeping along darkened corridors and sneaking into bedrooms they shouldn't be in?" Amanda laughed. "Sorry to disappoint you, inspector."

"Not exactly what I had in mind, Miss Laye," replied Constable severely. "I have rather more serious matters on my mind. Such as investigating the brutal murder of this country's Prime Minister."

Amanda's face grew instantly solemn. "Of course, inspector. I'm sorry. And be assured, if there was anything I could tell you that would help your investigation, I would do so. But there's nothing."

*

The door of the next bedroom along the corridor, unlike the ceramics of its predecessors, bore a brass plate in the shape of an elephant bearing the legend 'The Indian Bedroom' in pseudo-Hindi script. In response to the invitation to enter, the detectives were greeted by a surprising invocation of the Raj at the height of its glory. Wooden shutters in intricate fretted designs flanked the windows. Reliefs of snarling marble tigers supported the mantelshelf. Aristocratic bronze egrets formed the bases of lamps with red silk tasselled shades. Peacock feathers adorned the canopy of an impressive four-poster bed with swagged hangings of purple and gold. And, almost dwarfed by the large throne-like chair in which he sat, a man in his forties, who looked up enquiringly from the sheaf of papers in his hand.

"Sorry to disturb you, sir." Andy Constable introduced himself.

"Of course, of course." The man sprang to his feet and virtually bounded across the room, hand outstretched in greeting. He was short, almost verging on plump, with a shining face and dark hair, and he exuded an air of great energy. "Inspector ... sergeant." He pumped his visitors' hands vigorously. "What can I do to help you? Oh ... do sit down ... that's if you can find somewhere." He bustled to move piles of paperwork from the pair of chairs which flanked a marble-topped table inlaid with a floral design in multi-coloured stones, juggled with the breakfast tray it bore, flung the papers untidily on the bed, dislodging his red leather briefcase which crashed to the floor, waved a hand dismissively in its direction, and then resumed his seat with an expectant look.

Constable, slightly taken aback at the whirl of activity, drew breath. "I'm sure you appreciate that we need to gather as much information as we possibly can regarding the events leading up to this morning, sir." He paused, a slight frown creasing his brow. "Forgive me, sir, but I can't help feeling that our paths have crossed before. Have we met?"

The man laughed. "I get that a lot, inspector. As a politician, I'm not sure whether to be flattered at the recognition or depressed that people don't know who I am."

"But for the benefit of my sergeant's notes, sir ...," said Constable carefully.

"Lewis Stalker, sergeant. Secretary of State for Culture, Media and Sport," explained the man. "Which is why I'm forever popping up in television studios around the country, whenever somebody wants a comment on what the BBC is getting up to, or whatever the latest sporting scandal may be. I suppose the producers see me as some sort of man for all subjects. The only trouble as far as I'm concerned is that people are concentrating so much on the football story or the shock production at the National Theatre that they don't actually notice me as a person. Salutary, really. We politicians always tend to get above ourselves and take ourselves too seriously." A frank grin.

"That will be where I've seen you then, sir"

"Mind you," continued Lewis, "I dare say when this news breaks, my feet won't touch the floor. Every media outlet in the country will be on the phone to me like a shot. Not that it would do them much good at the moment, of course.

Phone confiscated yesterday by the formidable Inspector Deare. Evidently somebody doesn't trust me."

"Not just you, sir," said Constable. "I believe the inspector has taken charge of everybody's phone, on instructions from Mrs. Ronson. I think it was thought vital that information about this meeting should not leak out prematurely. And under the present circumstances, even more so."

"Understandable, I suppose," nodded Lewis. "Dodgy things, leaks."

"So if we may come back to the matter in hand, sir," prompted Constable.

Lewis shook his head. "It's inexplicable, Mr. Constable. To think that I was sitting next to Doris at dinner last night, having a perfectly normal conversation, and now she's dead. I suppose there's no idea who's done this?"

"Rather too early to say, sir. We're still gathering information. So, regarding yesterday, may I assume that you arrived here at more or less the same time as the rest of your colleagues?"

"I did."

"And I'm told there was some sort of gathering before the party left the Hall to go to dinner."

"That's right. Slightly surprising that the cars were all sent away, so we had to cram into just the two to get down to the village."

"Did you have any conversations with Mrs. Ronson at that point?"

"No, I was in the other car, squashed in the

back with three of the ladies. But as I said, I did sit next to her at dinner."

"And I don't suppose you can recall anything helpful that was said during the course of the meal," surmised Constable gloomily.

Lewis laughed. "Not really. It was intended to be a jolly social occasion with all shop-talk forbidden." He snorted. "Fat chance! That might have been the theory, but you could tell there were undercurrents. I mean, for instance, we got into the room and were shuffling about to choose our seats, and Dee Nye grabbed a chair at one end of the table like the queen bee she likes to think she is, and Marion Hayste couldn't get to the seat at the other end quick enough. Bit of status rivalry going on there, I thought. But it was mostly superficial. Mandy Laye and Erica Mayall were across the table from me, and the P.M. seemed more interested in talking to both of them about overseas trips. I wasn't paying that much attention, but I remember she mentioned one of Erica's jaunts to America to some conference on women's rights, and the conversation shot off on a tangent about designer shoes." He grew solemn. "Not really the sort of topic you expect to lead to someone getting killed."

"And you, sir? I'm guessing you didn't join in with the talk of ladies' footwear?"

"Not quite my scene, inspector. No, I got into the subject of handling the press with Perry Neal. He seemed quite intrigued as to how I manage to pull the strings to get the stories out that we want to tell, and how to sit on the people we don't much like. I used to be in P.R. in a previous incarnation, you see, and I think he regards it all as something of a dark art. I just told him it's mostly a case of knowing where all the bodies are buried." He stopped short. "And there I go again. That wasn't particularly tasteful, was it, inspector? I was always told that my big mouth would get me into trouble one day."

"But not with Mrs. Ronson, sir?"

"What?"

"Your meeting with her on your return to the Hall, sir," said Constable smoothly. "There were no tensions there?"

"Oh." A slightly disconcerted pause. "No, none at all. We mostly talked about the B.B.C., as I recall. And afterwards, I came straight up here because there was a football match on television, and I need to keep up to speed with who's winning what, or else I look a complete duffer when I'm interviewed on the Europa League or whatever." A candid smile.

"And you didn't leave your room after that?"

"No. The match went into extra time, and then penalties, so by the time the talking heads had finished pontificating, I was ready for the sack. I went out like a light."

"And heard nothing?"

"Not until this morning. Then Inspector Deare came knocking with the sad news, and I've been cooped up here ever since."

*

The door of the next room opened almost as soon as the sound of Andy Constable's knock had died away.

"Yes?" The woman who stood in the doorway of the Red Room was surprisingly young, scarcely past thirty in Constable's estimation, with brown hair curling just beyond her shoulders and large deep-blue eyes which would have been her most arresting feature, were it not for the dark circles under them which marred their attractiveness. "Oh. It's not ...." She seemed agitated.

"Our apologies, madam," said the inspector smoothly. "I hope I didn't startle you. Were you expecting someone?"

"No. Not at all. Well, perhaps Inspector Deare. I thought she might be coming to tell us ..." She tailed off.

"I'm sorry, madam, but I'm afraid you'll have to put up with me and my colleague." Constable and Copper showed their warrant cards with a few brief words of explanation. "I wonder if we might come in for a moment."

"Oh. Yes. You'd better sit down. I'm afraid there's only one chair."

"That's perfectly all right, madam," smiled Constable, with a sideways look at his junior. "Sergeant Copper is quite used to standing." He took a seat and glanced around the room, while its occupant paced restlessly. It was considerably smaller than the other bedrooms the detectives had visited – perhaps a lady's maid's room or a former dressing room, he surmised – and the lack of space was accentuated by the colour scheme, with walls covered in a dark red flocked paper, a tiny black cast-iron fireplace, and windows flanked by heavy maroon velvet curtains. "It makes it easier for him to concentrate on his note-taking. Perhaps he'd better start with your name."

"It's Marion – Marion Hayste."

"Ah yes. Mrs?" A nod. "Your name's been mentioned to us already."

"It has? I mean, how ...?"

"Your fellow-minister Mrs. Nye spoke of you when we talked to her a little while ago. I gather you came down to Dammett Hall together in her car."

"Yes. Yes, we did."

"Because I understand that you work together – am I right?"

"I work for her," said Marion. "I'm a minister in her department – Minister for Prisons, actually."

Constable couldn't stop his eyebrows rising in surprise. "That's a very heavy responsibility for anyone, madam. Let alone, if you don't mind me saying so, someone relatively young. I mean, there are some serious hardened criminals out there. And I should know."

Marion attempted a small smile. "You aren't the only one who's surprised at my appointment, inspector. I was fairly amazed myself, particularly since I was one of the new intake of M.P.s at the last election. But Mrs. Ronson said that she was determined to have fresh blood, and ..." Marion broke off at the import of her words, and her hand went to her mouth. "Oh dear."

"Would you like to sit down?" asked Constable in concerned tones, rising from his chair.

"No, no. I'm fine." Marion took a deep breath. "It's just all very upsetting. Killing someone like that – it's just so horrible."

"Which is why we need to get to the bottom of it as soon as we can, Mrs. Hayste. And so, if you're sure you are up to it, I do need to ask you some questions."

"Please, inspector, carry on." Marion seemed calmer.

"Were you aware of any tensions between any of your colleagues and Mrs. Ronson, either before or during yesterday's gathering?"

Marion shook her head. "Not that I can think of, inspector. I've only been in post a short while, and I'm afraid I'm still very junior, so I'm not quite au fait with everything that goes on."

"How about any conflicts between your fellow-ministers which might have spilt over?" hazarded Constable. "For instance, I gather you and Mrs. Nye had quite an animated conversation before everyone went off to the village for dinner."

"Did we?" Marion looked uncertain, but then her face cleared. "Oh, that. That was nothing, inspector. We were just talking about some initiative that I'm supposed to be implementing. Very dull government stuff."

"And did the conversation stay dull over dinner?"

"I'm afraid it did. Not that I took much of a part in it. I was sat between Lewis Stalker and Perry Neal, and Lew is never one to use one word where ten will do, so it was mostly a question of sitting back and letting the talk flow over me."

"And after dinner, everyone came back here for their series of meetings with the Prime Minister."

"That's right. And I had to wait around until everyone else had been in – the penalty for being the most junior member of the team, I suppose – so there was nothing to do but sit around and listen to other people making conversation. Thank goodness the bar had been left open, or we'd have all died of boredom." Marion closed her eyes at the import of her words.

Constable's attention was alerted. "So are you saying that you were the last person to see Mrs. Ronson last night, and everyone else had disappeared by the time you left?"

"Oh no, inspector. Perry was still in the drawing room when I came out from my meeting with the P.M. And I stayed and had a brief word with him, and Mrs. Ronson poked her head into the room while we were talking. I think she was quite surprised that we were still there. But then she said, rather pointedly I thought, that she wouldn't need either of us any more and that we were quite at liberty to go to bed."

"That sounds like a fairly firm dismissal."

"That's what we thought," said Marion. "We looked at one another, and Perry raised one eyebrow, the way he does, and then we made our way up here together." Constable gave a slightly quizzical look. "No, I don't mean together, not like that," explained the minister hurriedly. "I just mean ... he's in the next room, you see. His Lordship's Room." She gestured. "Much grander than the room they allocate to a mere Minister of State. As are most of the others."

"You ... er ... you've seen Dr. Neal's room?" enquired Constable carefully.

"No!" was Marion's swift reaction. "No. He just told me about it, that's all. So we said goodnight in the corridor and ... well, that was it, really."

"And did you hear anything after you retired? Any sounds of someone moving about the house, perhaps?"

"No, nothing."

"And you didn't leave the room yourself?"

"Why would I? Anyway, I haven't had any chance, have I? Inspector Deare came up with the news first thing and said that everyone was being asked to stay put, so that's what I've done. I haven't even been able to call my husband, and it's our wedding anniversary today."

*

Outside in the corridor once again, Andy Constable lowered his voice. "I hope you got all that, sergeant."

Dave Copper looked puzzled. "I think so, guv. I've made notes of pretty much everything she said."

"But what about what she didn't say?"

"How do you mean, guv?"

"Oh, all sorts of things. For example, according to her account, Mrs. Ronson seemed quite eager to get rid of the last two still downstairs after her string of meetings. What do you suppose that means?"

Copper cottoned on. "Right, guv. She was still expecting someone. One of the players was due to come back down again for a second session."

"That's what I took it to mean. But we have no idea who at the moment. And then there's the matter of that little door."

"What, the one going through to her bathroom? What about it?"

"Not that one, sergeant," smiled Constable. "The other one, obviously left over from when it was a servant's room. The one half-hidden behind that screen in the corner of the room. The one which almost blends into the wall because it's covered with the same wallpaper as the rest of the room. The one which leads through into the room next door ..."

"... which is occupied by the man with whom she seemed most anxious to deny that there was anything going on," grinned Copper. "Maybe that's why she's so jumpy. Illicit nookie in the corridors of power, despite what Amanda Laye said."

"Not quite how I would have put it," said Constable, "but it's one possible strand of thought. Does that sort of thing damage a politician's prospects these days?" He shrugged. "Perhaps we'll learn more from Mr. Neal himself."

Chapter 5

Dr. Peregrine Neal looked exactly like the sort of traditional family G.P. always portrayed in films or television programmes from the 1950s. Appearing to be in his early sixties, tweed-jacketed, tall and gangling with a slight stoop, he answered the knock at his door and inspected his visitors over the top of his half-frame spectacles.

"Mr. Neal?"

"Doctor, actually" came the gentle correction.

"I beg your pardon, sir. But you are Dr. Neal?"

"Yes. How can I help?"

"Detective Inspector Constable, sir. And this is my colleague, Detective Sergeant Copper. We've been charged with the initial investigation into the Prime Minister's death."

"Ah. Sheila Deare mentioned that you would be calling, inspector. You'd better come in." Perry Neal stood back to allow the detectives into the room, and waved them to a sofa placed in front of a large marble fireplace, while he took a seat in an armchair alongside it.

Constable looked around briefly. The room was a complete contrast to the one he had last visited. Spacious, dominated by a large half-tester bed with curtains in a bold regency stripe of green and gold, the atmosphere was subtly masculine, with furnishings including a classical Empire-style chiffonier, desk, and upright chairs, the walls decorated with large framed monochrome etchings of Palladian country houses and architectural details. The door which led to the previous adjoining room, the inspector noted, was also discreetly incorporated into the décor.

"Dr. Neal," began Constable, "you're familiar with the situation, I think."

"Of course."

"So I'm hoping you'll be able to help me with some additional information."

"What are you after, inspector? Full clinical details of how the Prime Minister met her end?"

"Our own doctor has already given us an idea as to that," replied Constable. He frowned. "Just a moment. Are you saying that you have seen the body?"

An infinitesimal pause. "Certainly not, inspector. No, the instructions were quite clear when Inspector Deare came round this morning – nobody was to leave their room, so of course I sat tight in here. However much professional interest and plain human curiosity might have been calling me downstairs to examine the P.M. No, I resisted the temptation and caught up with the latest in The Lancet instead. In my position, I have to keep my finger on the pulse." Perry winced. "My apologies, inspector. That was a very old medic's joke from a very old medic. I'm afraid I still can't manage to avoid the old consulting room humour."

"Are you saying you're still practising, doctor?" enquired Constable, surprised.

"Hardly," said Perry. "My surgeries these days are political rather than medical. Much as I might like to keep my hand in, but it's not really compatible with being Secretary of State for Health. Too much passing across my desk. But I still can't seem to shake off the habit of taking my bag with me wherever I go. Because you never know, do you?" He gestured to the traditional black doctor's bag lying at the foot of the bed. "After all, it's only around two years since it was my daily companion."

"Really, sir? How so?"

"That was when I first got elected, at the by-election. There was quite a bit about it in the papers at the time."

Memories stirred at the back of Constable's mind. "Of course, sir. You were the surprise victor, weren't you?"

"That's right. I'd stood as an Independent in support of the local hospital because there was a great row at the time about the possibility of its closure, and somehow, against all the odds, people decided to vote for me, and I won the seat. Trumped all expectations, you might say. And then, after the last election, Mrs. Ronson decided that she wanted somebody with proper hands-on experience to run the Health Department, so she gave it to me."

"Something of a meteoric rise, sir," commented Constable.

"As you say, inspector. I've had to learn the game of politics at breakneck speed. So now I am the one who has to make all the difficult decisions about financial strictures and possible hospital closures, which means that I have begun to have a sneaking sense of sympathy for my predecessor."

"And was this the burden of your talks with the Prime Minister during your meeting last night, sir?" Constable sought to return the conversation to the matter in hand.

Perry shrugged. "Partly. Not really in any detail. In fact, our chat was all fairly general. I can't think of anything that stood out. Mind you, by then I imagine the P.M. was getting pretty tired. I know I was, and I was the last but one in. There was only Marion after me. And when I came out, everyone else had vanished, so I just had a nightcap before coming up to bed. In fact, I think I may have dozed off for a moment, but I managed to pretend to be awake when Marion came out, and then shortly after that, we both came up, leaving the place deserted."

"No indications while you were waiting while everyone else had their interviews with Mrs. Ronson that there might be any tensions in the wind, doctor?" asked Constable, more in hope than expectation. "No remarks – tight lips – angry expressions?"

"You're looking for someone who emerged from their meeting snarling revenge, inspector?" said Perry with a smile. "You have to remember that, unlike me, most of these people are professional politicians. Hiding their feelings is what they do best."

*

"I have an inkling," murmured Andy Constable to Dave Copper as the two stood outside the door of the next bedroom along the corridor, "that the bluff Dr. Neal is not quite the candid innocent he would like us to believe."

"I'll tell you one thing that struck me, guv," returned Dave Copper. "That bit about not having seen Mrs. Ronson's body. He was pretty quick to say he hadn't, but not quite quick enough, and there was a bit of wriggly body language that made me wonder."

"Two minds with but a single thought," agreed Constable, "but exactly what that implies will have to wait. For now, let's see who's occupying ..." He consulted the plaque on the door. "... the State Bedroom."

To say that the room was grand would be to understate the facts. Every corner dripped with decoration. Dominated by an enormous four-poster bed, brocade-hung and topped with explosions of ostrich plumes at the corners and a central golden coronet, the room glinted with gilt and glass, and formed a suitably opulent setting for the woman who responded to the detectives' knock with a languid 'Come in!', as she lounged elegantly on the Georgian sofa at the foot of the bed. Her appearance had a touch of the exotic – her skin tones were warm, her hair jet black and glossy, and her enormous dark eyes surveyed her visitors with a hint of challenge.

"Forgive the interruption, Mrs. ...?"
"Ms."
"I'm sorry ... Ms. ...?"

"Mayall. Erica Mayall. And you are ...?"

"Detective Inspector Constable." Constable, slightly disconcerted, fumbled for his credentials, and nudged his colleague to do likewise. "I've been ordered to investigate the matter of the sudden death of the Prime Minister, and I'm beginning by speaking to everyone who was in the house last night. I hope this isn't an inconvenient moment."

"No more than any other, inspector." Erica rose, wrapped her long silk robe, embroidered with fantastical dragons, a little more firmly around herself, and swayed across the room to pour herself a cup of coffee from her otherwise seemingly untouched breakfast tray. She did not offer any to her visitors. Coffee in hand, she perched on the stool of her dressing table while waving the other hand vaguely in the direction of the sofa she had just vacated. She raised her finely sculpted eyebrows expectantly. "Well?"

"This is a magnificent room, Ms. Mayall," said Constable, declining to be intimidated by the slightly confrontational atmosphere.

"The best in the house, actually." Erica was unable to conceal a note of self-satisfaction.

"Anyone might have thought that this would have been reserved for the Prime Minister, rather than one of her more junior colleagues," suggested Constable.

"Oh, it was probably just the luck of the draw," replied Erica airily. "And Doris was perfectly happy for me to have this room. She said it all looked rather too froufrou for her tastes."

"I can see that," said Constable easily, surveying the décor. "I must say, if it were me, I'd also prefer something rather more masculine. So, I take it you were close, you and the P.M.?"

"I'm sorry? What exactly do you mean, inspector?" There was an unexpected hint of hostility.

"I simply mean, were you particularly close colleagues? I gather that it's not always easy having genuine friendships in politics."

"Well, I suppose we may have been closer than many. We did come into the House of Commons at the same time, a couple of elections back, and we shared an office for a while when we were both on the opposition benches. And, of course, as a woman Prime Minister, she was intensely interested in my portfolio."

Constable gave an apologetic smile. "Forgive me, Ms. Mayall, but I'm afraid I'm not one hundred percent up to speed with what everyone does. And unfortunately the nature of your ministerial job has so far escaped me."

"How like a man," retorted Erica waspishly. "I am the Secretary of State for Women's Affairs, inspector. I think you'll find that my ministry is destined to be one of the more important ones in the future."

"Despite the talk I've heard that one of the reasons for this gathering of ministers might have foreshadowed a re-shuffle? You had no concerns for your own future on that score?"

"None whatsoever." The response was swift

and frosty.

"You had no areas of conflict with Mrs. Ronson?"

"As I said, Mr. Constable, none. How often would you like me to repeat it?"

"And how about your other colleagues, Ms. Mayall? After all, I am afraid that there is no denying the fact that either you or one of your colleagues has killed our country's Prime Minister."

Erica bit her lip. "Must you be so brutal, inspector?" She closed her eyes for a moment and sighed. When she resumed, her voice was softer. "No, I have no idea why anyone would do such a thing."

Constable glanced at his junior. "Copper, correct me, but I think that Ms. Mayall was in the other car, not Mrs. Ronson's, when the party adjourned to the village for dinner?"

A brief riffle of the pages of Copper's notebook. "That's right, sir. Together with Miss Laye, Mr. Stalker, Mrs. Nye and Dr. Neal."

"I just wondered if there was anything said during the journey, or over dinner, that might give me a pointer towards any tensions in the party." Constable looked enquiringly at the minister.

Erica shook her head. "Nothing that seems relevant, inspector. And Lewis and Perry were so busy dominating the conversation at dinner that it was difficult to get a word in edgeways. I exchanged a few words with Doris and Mandy, but nothing that would help you, I think."

"Nothing significant in the talk about shoes, then?" smiled Constable.

"I don't know what you mean by that." Erica shifted slightly, and there was a sharpness in her tone which surprised the inspector.

"Nothing in particular, Ms. Mayall. I was just remembering a snippet of your conversation which someone overheard. That's all."

"Oh. I see." Erica gave a small and slightly false laugh. "No, that was just girl talk."

"As one might expect from a government minister in charge of policy regarding women's affairs." Constable risked a small jibe, moving swiftly on before Erica could react. "And when the party returned here to the Hall, I suppose nothing emerged from the individual meetings you all had with Mrs. Ronson?"

"Everything was completely confidential, inspector. The P.M. made that perfectly clear to all of us, I think. Certainly nobody said anything to me." She thought for a moment. "I was about halfway down the list, I suppose. Yes, because Milo had his session before me, and Benny followed on after me."

"Benny?"

"Benjamin Fitt. The Social Security Secretary. He's in the room next door to this one."

"Which means that we shall be speaking to him shortly, Ms Mayall." Constable got to his feet. "Perhaps he'll be able to give us more information as to anything that may have happened later."

Erica shrugged. "Maybe. I certainly can't. I went out to the front door because I wanted to go out for a breath of air, but then I found that we'd all been locked in, and there was no sign of the manager to let me out, so I just came up here and read a magazine."

"You saw no-one else after that? And no-one else saw you?"

Erica gave a cat-like smile. "Wanting an alibi, inspector? Sorry, but I'm afraid I can't provide one. And after last night's sessions, I doubt if anyone else can. Probably all too busy licking their wounds in private after the P.M. had finished with them."

*

"What on earth do you reckon she meant by that last remark, guv?" enquired Dave Copper in a discreet undertone as he closed the door of the State Bedroom behind him.

"I think that she has perhaps confirmed what we probably already suspected," replied Andy Constable. "In other words, that everything that we've been told about light inconsequential chats about nothing in particular between Mrs. Ronson and her ministers is just a load of old guff. If there was nothing more important to discuss than football coverage and fashions in footwear, it could all have been done over a glass of government-issue sherry in Downing Street."

"Yes, but nobody's told us anything helpful yet on that score, have they, guv?"

"They will in time, Copper. Just trust the old adage – the more people talk, the more they give themselves away. And don't forget, we've got a few overheard snippets, which I'm willing to bet will bear closer inspection, if past experience is anything to go by. So, let us speak to this Mr. Fitt, who if my calculations are correct, is the last one in our parade of ministers."

Copper checked his notebook. "He is, sir." He grinned. "The last of our wise monkeys, all busy seeing, hearing, and speaking no evil. Ah, but what about 'doing no evil'?"

"That, sergeant," said Constable with an answering smile, "we shall discover." He tapped on the door, which bore the legend 'The Cedar Room', and in response to the cheery 'Come in' from within, entered the room.

A large window gave spectacular views across the lawns leading down to the lake, with the prospect graced by the enormous cedar tree which lent the room its name. Delicately carved wooden panelling featuring a profusion of birds, fruits, and foliage adorned the walls, and the theme was continued with a suite of delicate eighteenth-century furniture which Constable surmised could quite easily be genuine Chippendale.

The sophisticated atmosphere of the room was in complete contrast to its occupant, who virtually bounced across the floor to greet the detectives. He was short and round-faced, reminiscent of an eager bulldog pup, plump of frame but quick in his movements. His age could have been anywhere in the forties or fifties.

"At long last!" he cried. "The Old Bill has

finally arrived! I've been sat here waiting for you to turn up for ages." The voice made no compromises – the accent was pure East End of London, with a rasp which hinted at a history of heavy smoking.

"Mr. Benjamin Fitt?" enquired Constable.

"That's right," confirmed the man. "But for goodness sake, call me Benny. Everyone else has, ever since I was a kid. Well, I say everyone. I can't get some of this lot to do it." A nod of the head to indicate his colleagues in the rest of the house. "Too stuck in formality for their own good. In my opinion, they've all got their heads shoved too far up their own ... well, you get the idea."

"I think I do, Mr. Fitt," said Constable, amused almost against his will. "But if you don't mind, considering the circumstances, I think I'd prefer to be a little more formal in my approach."

"Fine by me. Okay, grab a seat." Benny threw himself into a chair while the detectives, after a slightly uncertain pause, perched on a spindly-looking sofa. "So, you're the forces of law and order, sent to sort out this kerfuffle?"

"As you say, sir. Detective Inspector Constable, and my colleague here is Detective Sergeant Copper." The two produced their identification.

Benny scarcely glanced at it. "Sheila Deare said you'd be along." He looked at his watch. "She didn't say you'd be quite so long about it."

"Apologies for keeping you waiting, sir," replied Constable. "But we have had quite a number of your colleagues to interview, and it just so happened that you were the final one."

"Bit of a bugbear of mine, waiting times," remarked Benny. "Keeping people hanging about waiting to be seen is one of the things I'm trying to get a handle on."

"Sir?"

"In my Department," explained Benny. "Social Security, in case you didn't know. People pitch up with their problems, and then they're kept waiting around while my staff fight the computer system. I said to the P.M., we have to get it sorted if it kills us." He grimaced. "I didn't mean it quite so literally." He drew a breath. "Anyway, my computers are nothing to do with why you're here. You'll be wanting to sort out this business with Doris."

"And any help you can give us will be much appreciated, sir."

Benny leaned forward in his chair. "Ask away."

"I suppose we'd better begin with the lead-up to this meeting of the Prime Minister's, sir. Would you have any idea why you might have been included in the group, while some of your fellow-ministers were not?"

"Not a clue, inspector." Benny's expression was candid. "Maybe Doris wanted to discuss some of my new ideas. They're not to everyone's liking, but then, I'm not that much of a politician."

"No, sir?"

Benny snorted. "Well, not a party politician, anyway. I came up through the trade unions. Not quite born with a silver spoon in my mouth. There weren't that many around in the part of Whitechapel where I grew up. As you can probably tell from the accent."

"I guessed it might be somewhere like that, sir. I imagine that might account for your interest in the work of your Department. They're very strong on family values in that neck of the woods, aren't they?"

Benny suddenly looked unaccountably wary. "What are you saying, inspector?"

"Oh, I'm not trying to prise any policy secrets out of you, minister," said Constable hastily. "No, it's just that I remember somebody mentioned that they'd heard part of a conversation between yourself and the Prime Minister over dinner about the importance of families, that's all."

"Oh, I see." Benny relaxed slightly. "Anyway, you wanted to talk about how this set-up all came about, didn't you?"

Constable nodded. "Some background information never goes amiss, sir."

"Depends how far back you want to go, inspector. Okay, brief history of Benny Fitt. Left school the minute I could, got into the transport union, worked my way up, got selected in a by-election for a parliamentary constituency in the Midlands ..."

"Not London, sir. Not where your roots were? I'm surprised."

"No, I got out of there years ago," said Benny. "Anyway, I got elected. That was when my old party was in opposition. But then after all this rigmarole over the past year or two, when the new party got formed and we won, Doris called me up and said she wanted to make me a minister. Bit of a turn-up, I thought, but you don't look a gift horse in the mouth, so I grabbed it. And here I am."

"With a number of people you never expected to have as close colleagues, I'm guessing, sir," suggested Constable.

"You're right there, inspector," agreed Benny with a wry grin. "They reckon politics makes for strange bed-fellows."

"And do you find yourself among strange bed-fellows, Mr. Fitt?"

Benny gave him a look. "Not sure exactly what you're asking, inspector. I don't do gossip. But if you mean, did we all start out singing from the same hymn sheet, then I'd have to say no, not by a long chalk."

"Which might easily have led to tensions between colleagues, sir," said Constable. "Any in particular that strike you as relevant to the Prime Minister's death?"

"You mean ... hang on. You're saying that one of us lot is the one that killed her? Oh, you've got to be kidding."

"There's no other possible explanation, sir. This house was a secure environment last night – there was no opportunity for anyone to enter or leave. It has to be one of the party."

"Blimey." Benny sat back and whistled in surprise. "You know, I'd never twigged that that was the reason for all this staying-put-in-our-rooms malarkey. So ..." He paused in thought. "That's what you're getting at. You reckon someone who sat down to dinner last night ended up sticking the knife into Doris? Well ... that is politics with a vengeance."

Chapter 6

"Guv." Dave Copper sounded excited as the detectives paused at the top of the stairs. "You don't suppose that bit about sticking the knife in was a bit of a giveaway, do you? I mean, how many people know that Mrs. Ronson was stabbed?"

"I really couldn't say, sergeant," replied Andy Constable. "It could have been just a figure of speech. And we don't know what Inspector Deare has told all these people in explanation. Maybe I should have warned her about the hazards of being too free with information, because you never know when someone is going to let slip something that ends up incriminating them. My fault for not thinking of it - I dare say she's not as used as we are to wallowing around in the murky waters of sudden death. Well, not much point in worrying about that now."

"No use crying over spilt blood, eh, guv?"

"And we're back in the world of the off-colour Copper remark," sighed Constable. "I thought you'd been unusually quiet for a while. Have you been spending your time thinking that up instead of doing your job and noting everything we've been told?"

"No, guv, honestly," protested Copper. He brandished his notebook in evidence. "Pages and pages of stuff. One thing about politicians, they can't half talk."

"Just be grateful that we've only got this

relatively few to deal with," returned Constable. "If it had been the full cabinet, you'd have had over twice as many to deal with, and we'd have been here forever."

"Grateful for small mercies, as ever, sir," grinned Copper. "So, what now? Back downstairs and carry on?"

"Not just yet, sergeant. We still have one thing to do up here. I want to check through the Prime Minister's room. I think we were put on the right track when we were told that there was a re-shuffle in the wind. Maybe the people here were licking their wounds, as Ms. Mayall put it, because they were all potentially in line for the chop."

"And one of them got their chop in first, guv?"

"As you say. And there's one factor that nobody's mentioned yet."

"What's that, guv?"

"Ambition. The Prime Minister's dead. Someone is going to have to take her place. Why shouldn't one of these people believe that they would be the appropriate successor?"

"Bit far-fetched, isn't it, guv?"

Constable raised his eyebrows. "What, and this whole situation isn't? I suspect we can't rule anything out. Anyway, I want to go through Mrs. Ronson's things. You never know, there may be something helpful."

"Are we allowed to go poking about in state secrets, guv? Couldn't that get us into trouble?"

"What, and you think there's a bigger state

secret than the one we're sitting on top of?" scoffed Constable. "The Prime Minister's lying downstairs in a pool of blood, and it looks as if she's been murdered by one of her own cabinet colleagues. I think, at the moment, anything else, other than the nuclear launch codes, is probably fairly insignificant. So, back to the Chinese Bedroom."

*

The Prime Minister's room wore a faintly expectant air, as if it anticipated the return of its occupant at any moment to resume normal life. The door of a large black lacquered wardrobe stood slightly ajar, giving a glimpse of the rail of clothing hanging inside. A pair of shoes lay haphazard under a chair, evidently discarded in favour of a preferred choice. A brief glance through the open door of the marble-clad en-suite bathroom revealed nothing more interesting than an extensive array of dazzling white opulent towels and a contrastingly modest selection of personal cosmetics in a simple black leather wash-bag.

"Where to start then, guv?" queried Dave Copper.

"Oh, the usual routine, I think," said Andy Constable. "You can prowl the room top to bottom, while I seat myself in comfort in this armchair and see if there's anything to be found amongst the paperwork which I can see sitting invitingly in the despatch box on the bed."

"Are you sure you're allowed to do that, guv? I mean, confidential government papers and all that. We don't want to find ourselves on the wrong end of a charge for contravening the Official Secrets Act, do we?"

"You let me worry about that, sergeant," replied Constable, moving his chair to within easy reach of the foot of the bed. "As far as you're concerned, you're just following the orders of your superior officer. And as far as I'm concerned, nothing is going to stop me getting on with a murder investigation. And if the lady didn't see fit to lock her case, I can't see that we're going to be the ones in trouble for looking inside." He pulled the briefcase towards him and began to examine the contents.

The first item to hand was a substantial file, whose cover bore the crowned portcullis symbol of the House of Commons and the portentous title 'Public Accounts Committee – Abuses of the Expenses System'.

"Oh, not again," thought Constable. He opened the file and glanced at the contents page. There were cross-references to lists of names of Members of Parliament, as well as various functionaries of the House, with sub-headings regarding personal expenses, employment of staff, and expenditure incurred in the performance of official duties. Page after page of columns followed, with comments, footnotes, and occasional conclusions highlighted in bold type. Constable groaned. "This is going to take forever to go through," he thought. "But there has to be something relevant here, or else why has Mrs. Ronson bothered to have this particular file with her for this particular set of meetings?" He laid the file aside and looked further into the briefcase.

Lying beneath the file was an imposing book, about the size of a substantial photograph album, bound in purple leather adorned with embossed gold leaf. On opening it, Constable was surprised to discover that it was the hotel's register. In a large colour photograph on the first inside page, a slightly sheepish Phil Knightly formed one of a group of dignitaries on the steps of Dammett Hall, prominently fronted by a middle-aged woman wearing a floating summer dress and a striking picture hat, holding in one hand an extravagant bouquet of flowers, and in the other a large pair of golden scissors. Evidently the official opening ceremony of the hotel, surmised the inspector. The following pages were laid out as a combination of conventional register and traditional country-house visitors book – there was a list of dates of arrival, names and addresses, sometimes in the most abbreviated form, with spaces for the occasional comment, mostly fulsome, from satisfied guests on departure. Turning to the most recent entries, Constable read the list of the latest arrivals, headed by the confident sprawling hand of 'Doris Ronson, 10 Downing Street, SW1', followed by all her ministerial colleagues in scripts ranging from the most fastidious copperplate to the virtually illegible. What on earth, Constable wondered, is the Prime Minister doing with the hotel register in her possession? Surely she's perfectly well aware of who is on the premises with her. Or is there something in the narrative of the building since it became a hotel which interests her? Something else which will need to be trawled through.

A small and rather battered-looking brown leather notebook, similar to that in which Copper had been making his copious notes, came next to hand. Held closed with an elastic band, it had evidently seen long service. Constable opened it carefully, conscious of the slightly ominous cracking sound from the spine of the book, and flicked through a seemingly random collection of names and phone numbers, many of them apparently of long standing, with amendments made over many years, together with notes of meetings and their conclusions, remarks on individuals, some of whom were prominent personalities and many of whom were utterly unfamiliar. There seemed to be no pattern – the book looked to be an ad hoc record of Doris Ronson's political progress, and, it occurred to the inspector, would probably be a gold mine of information for anyone contemplating writing an autobiography. A little late for that, thought Constable with a grimace. It will have to be a biography now. As he was about to close the book, a small piece of paper fluttered from between the pages. Curious, Constable picked it up from the floor. Written on one of the hotel's compliments slips, in what was clearly not the Prime Ministerial hand, was the somewhat mysterious legend 'Not everyone is what they appear to be. S.D?'. Why would the P.M.'s security officer be writing her oblique notes, mused the inspector. Wouldn't it be simpler to find a moment to speak to her directly? And is this an implication that one of these ministers is lining themselves up, under a guise of friendly loyalty, to undertake some sort of a coup to oust the Prime Minister? Or worse?

Constable turned his attention to a small folded piece of paper which had been lying under the book. He unfolded it, to discover another example of the hotel's compliment slips. Why can't people use their own stationery, he thought, frustrated. It would make the authorship of these notes a great deal plainer. But at least this was clearly signed, although in a hand which did not match any of the other examples. It read 'My dearest Nymph, I must speak with you. Heather'. Nymph?? And who on earth is Heather, wondered the inspector.

Constable leafed briefly through the few remaining papers in the case. There seemed to be nothing of significance. A memo from one of the other ministries, not represented at the meeting, concerning a forthcoming set of trade talks. A note referring to the timetable for a suggested visit by the Prime Minister of one of the Commonwealth countries. A newspaper cutting of an article on drugs in inner city estates. And briefing notes relating to the impending conference of the Mothers' Institute, where a speech would be expected. As he was about to close the case, Constable noticed, tucked into a corner and almost invisible beneath the papers, a computer memory stick. He picked it up. Handwritten on it in cramped letters were the words 'The Nightly Politics – that interview'. The inspector was about to replace the stick, when something about the wording struck him. Not 'the interview' – perhaps a simple record of a broadcast which Mrs. Ronson had done recently, and which she might have wanted to review. No. 'That interview'. Evidently there was an air of notoriety about it. So was it by Mrs. Ronson herself, or perhaps by one of the ministers gathered together for the current meeting? And if so, did it provide fuel for concerns about someone's future career? The stick would need to be played to provide an answer. Something else which needed time, and Constable was acutely aware that, under present circumstances, this was a commodity in short supply. He pocketed the stick.

With a slight sigh of resignation, the inspector abandoned the briefcase and looked up, to see his junior colleague, a crumpled paper in his hand, on his knees alongside a small writing desk which stood in an alcove alongside the chimney breast. "What on earth are you doing grovelling about on the floor, sergeant?" he enquired.

Dave Copper picked himself up. "Just taking you at your word, guv," he responded cheerily. "You said do the room 'top to bottom', so that's what I've done. Not that it's been all that productive, mostly. Nothing in the wardrobes except a few clothes hanging up, and about the most exciting thing in there was one of Mrs. Ronson's coats in some horrible lime green colour. There ought to be a law against colours like that – it could put you right off your lunch." A level stare from his superior encouraged him to hurry on. "Anyway, nothing in any of the pockets. And there weren't even any handbags to rummage through. I'd have thought they were an essential accessory for a woman prime minister – didn't they always used to talk about people getting handbagged in the old days? Anyway, nothing there, and nothing in the luggage either, apart from a pretty strong smell of new leather. Somebody had very expensive tastes in suitcases. Monogrammed, too."

"Never mind the suitcases," said Constable. "It's baggage of the other kind that we're on the lookout for – either relating to the Prime Minister herself, or one of these other people, that might put us on the track of who'd have a motive to kill her."

"Sorry to disappoint, guv," said Copper. "I've been through the chest of drawers – nothing incriminating tucked away among the underwear. No dodgy substances in her cosmetics bag, as far as I can tell. And I was just finishing up by taking a look at the desk, but there weren't any of Mrs. Ronson's papers there – it looks as if you've got them all there in her briefcase. But ..."

"So, as you say, not all that productive." Constable stopped. A thought struck him, and his eye fell on the paper in his colleague's hand. "Just a minute. You said 'mostly'." He frowned slightly at the grin which spread slowly across Copper's face. "Come on, sergeant. Don't play games. Out with it. What's the 'But'? You've obviously got something."

"Sorry, guv." The grin broke out into a broad smile. "Couldn't resist it. But I think I've saved the best for last. And I almost missed it. It had obviously been chucked into the waste-paper bin under the desk, but it had missed and fallen into the gap behind. But I think you'll like it."

"So what is it?" Constable held out his hand.

Copper passed the crumpled sheet of paper across. "I only got a quick glance at it, guv, but it looks like the draft of a letter."

Constable took the sheet and smoothed it out on the top of the briefcase, while Copper moved to stand behind him to read over his shoulder. The paper was a sheet of the hotel's headed notepaper, evidently extracted from the leather folder on the desk.

"That's a scrawl and a half, isn't it, guv?" remarked the sergeant, as the pair surveyed the bold script littered with amendments and crossings-out.

"That's as may be, but the good thing is, it's definitely Mrs. Ronson's scrawl," replied the inspector. "It matches her handwriting in the hotel register. So, let's see what it's all about." He bent his head to peruse the letter's contents.

"'It is with some regret that I accept your

resignation' ," he read aloud. "Well, that's clear enough. Somebody was on the way out."

"Except that we don't know who, sir, do we? It's not addressed."

"Patience, sergeant. We may find out if we read on. 'Although we have ...' ... there's some crossing out here, so it's not that easy to read, but it looks like 'been close', but then that's been changed to 'known each other', but then that's been crossed out as well, and she's finally settled on 'worked together for many years, I agree that, in the event of the latest ...' there's a word here, but it's been pretty much scribbled over ... it might be 'startling' ... 'revelations, I believe there is no alternative.'"

"Startling revelations, eh, guv?" smiled Copper. "Everybody's been telling us how hunky-dory everything is. Are we starting to get somewhere?"

"Let's hope so." Constable browsed further. "Unfortunately, it doesn't look as if it's going to go into specifics ... 'good of the government's image', but then 'image' has been crossed out and replaced by 'reputation' ... 'need to be seen to be above criticism', but then she's deleted that and inserted 'reproach' ..." The inspector leaned back and sighed. "No, it doesn't look as if it's going to give us any clue as to who all this is referring to. And then it breaks off halfway through a sentence, and it's obviously been screwed up and thrown in the bin. Well, near it. But the question that prompts is, why?"

Copper shrugged. "Could be any number of

reasons, guv. Maybe Mrs. Ronson thought better of it and decided she wasn't going to accept the resignation of whoever-it-was after all. Maybe they thought that they could keep the lid on these startling revelations, whatever they were, if they hadn't actually got out yet. Or maybe she just decided that she didn't like what she'd written, what with all the crossings-out and all, and wanted to start again from scratch. It just so happened that she never got round to it, because there's no follow-up draft. Or ... here's another thought, guv. What if whoever wrote the resignation letter ..."

"Which seems to have vanished," interrupted Constable. "That's if there was a letter at all. There might well not have been. It could have been verbal."

"Be that as it may, sir," persisted Copper, "the person involved could have turned up at the door, and Mrs. Ronson might have chucked the draft away so that they didn't see what she was about. Although ..." He reflected for a moment. "Actually, it might have been anybody turning up, and she might still not have wanted them to see what she was about." He gave a grunt of annoyance. "Rats!"

"Too many maybes," snorted Constable in exasperation. "Too many whoevers and whatevers. And the other thought that occurs to me is, if this mysterious putative visitor does exist, did they take away with them this theoretical resignation letter and its theoretical reply? And, if not for the obvious reason that it was about themselves, why?" He ran his fingers through his hair. "This could drive a person crazy. I feel as if I'm trying to swim in treacle."

There was silence for a few seconds. "Can I make a suggestion, sir?" ventured Copper tentatively.

"All helpful suggestions gratefully received, sergeant," said Constable, leaning back and letting out a gusty sigh.

"Why don't we try a change of tack and go back to doing what we do best?"

"Which is?"

"Talk to people, guv. You've always told me that the best way to get to the bottom of things is to let people talk, and sooner or later the information you've been after slips out."

Constable rewarded his colleague with a smile of approval. "You're absolutely right, Copper. I'm glad you've been paying attention over all these years. Sound advice." He chuckled. "Except that I never expected to be on the receiving end of it from you. What's that line from the song – from *'The King and I'*, I think it is – 'by your pupils you'll be taught'."

"I don't know about that, guv." Copper looked faintly abashed. "But what do you reckon to the idea?"

Constable heaved himself to his feet. "I think it's a very good one."

"I mean, there's the people down at the village pub," continued Copper. "Old Gideon and so on. From all I remember, he was a cheery old bloke, so with a bit of luck, he'll lighten the mood a bit. Plus, when we were here before, he seemed to have his finger pretty much on the pulse of everything that was going on, so if he can't throw a bit of light on what happened during the dinner all this lot went to, I'd be surprised."

"You may well be right," replied Constable, his good humour restored, as he started for the door. "And there was also mention of a waitress, so we'll see if she can contribute anything." He stopped short. "Ah. That reminds me. There's one person on the premises we haven't yet got round to, and that's this waiter chap, or whatever he is, from the Downing Street staff. He's still cooling his heels downstairs in the morning room. We'll talk to him first before we go off charging round the countryside." He glanced at his watch. "And we'd better get on with it. Time's a-wasting." He strode briskly out of the room towards the stairs.

Chapter 7

At the foot of the stairs, the detectives headed to the left and, bypassing the library, pushed open the door to the morning room, to find a solitary occupant, feet up on a chesterfield sofa, leaning to pour himself a cup of coffee from the silver pot on the small wine table alongside him. He was a young man – late twenties, Constable gauged – slim, with a mop of dark hair falling forward over his forehead and sharp lively features enhanced by a pair of piercing blue eyes. He swung his feet to the floor and stood.

"Aha! At long last! You'll be the forces of law and order, if I'm not much mistaken." The voice rang with the broad distinctive accent of Belfast.

"You're absolutely right, sir," responded the inspector. "My name is Detective Inspector Constable, and my colleague here is Detective Sergeant Copper."

"Sheila said you'd be along. Although she didn't say you'd be this long about it. Good job I had the sense to fortify myself with some provisions." A nod towards a crumb-dotted plate among the coffee things.

"I'm afraid we've had quite a number of people to speak to so far this morning, sir," said Constable, a faint irritation in his tone. "It's just unfortunate that you happen to be at the end of my list. But you'll understand that I need to ask you some questions about this morning's events."

"Events, is it? Well, that's one way of putting it, I suppose. You'd better take a seat and get on with it, then." The man swung his feet back up on to the sofa, waving vaguely in the direction of a pair of armchairs alongside the fireplace. "I'd offer you a coffee, but I'm afraid I've just finished the last of it, and I dare say you haven't got the time for me to go and make a fresh pot." An open smile.

"I think I'd prefer to make a start, sir," said Constable, with a touch of grim determination. "Sergeant, perhaps you'd like to make some notes."

"Oh, on the record, is it?" The man composed his features into a serious expression, somewhat belied by the twinkle which remained in his eyes.

"It is, sir. Considering the circumstances. So I think we'll start with your name."

"Jim Daly, inspector."

"Would that be short for 'James', sir?" put in Copper, pen poised.

"Actually, no, sergeant. On the birth certificate it says 'Seamus', but everyone calls me Jim."

"Seamus Daly ..." murmured Copper in an undertone as he wrote.

"And that's 'Seamus' the proper Irish way, sergeant," said Jim. "None of your 'S... H... A...' nonsense."

"Got that, sir."

"And you're employed as a member of the catering staff at Number 10 Downing Street?" resumed Constable.

"Well, I have been. Who knows if I've still got a job, now that poor old DiDo's kicked the bucket."

Constable frowned in puzzlement. "Sorry, sir. What did you say?"

"DiDo, inspector. The Prime Minister." Jim raised his eyebrows at the inspector's continuing bafflement. "Oh, come on. Don't say you've not heard her called that before."

Constable turned to Copper with a querying look. "Sergeant, help me out here."

"I think it's what some of the papers call Mrs. Ronson, sir."

"Not the papers I read."

"Mostly the tabloids, I think, sir. Di Do, you see. Short for 'Diamond Doris'. Makes for a snappier headline, I suppose."

"I thought you weren't particularly interested in politics."

"Some people leave the papers lying around in the locker room at the station, sir," explained Copper defensively. "I just see the headlines. I don't actually read them."

"Well, I'm glad we've got that cleared up," said Constable heavily. "So, as you say, somewhat disrespectfully, Mr. Daly, the Prime Minister has been killed. And I've been put in charge of the immediate efforts to discover why and by whom."

"And you want to know what I know."

"Exactly, sir."

"Well, the short answer to that, inspector, is 'not a lot'."

"But you were in the house when the body was discovered, I think, Mr. Daly."

"In the house, yes. In the room, no. I'd only just got here this morning with Sheila Deare, so that I could get on with doing the breakfast, but it was that Knightly chap who actually went into the library and discovered the grisly corpse. At least, I assume it was grisly, because he came straight out again like a cork from a bottle, looking as white as the proverbial, and told us what he'd found. At which point Sheila snapped into action and took control. She went into the library to check what was what, and then out she came and told me to get into the kitchen and stay there while she got in touch with the higher-ups back in Whitehall. Do nothing, say nothing, touch nothing – those were her instructions, so I sat there like a lemon, until the orders changed and I got shunted in here, with hardly a second to grab myself something to keep the wolf from the door. And here you find me, not having seen a soul. And that's the whole story."

"Very concise, Mr. Daly," commented Constable. "And it ties in admirably with what we've already been told. But of course, it isn't the whole story, is it?"

"Is it not, inspector?"

"Not quite, Mr. Daly. Because we have yesterday evening to consider. I'm hoping you may be able to tell us something about what went on then."

"Not that I was around for most of it," said Jim. "After they'd had their dinner down at the pub, I stayed put down there while everyone else came back up here. So whatever they got up to after that, I don't know about it. Unfortunately. I wish I did."

"It would certainly help us if you did, sir. But as it is, we'll concentrate on the area where you may be able to help us, and that's during the dinner itself. You helped to serve, I understand."

"I did that, inspector."

"So perhaps some of the conversations at table, which I imagine you might well have overheard, could shed some light."

Jim burst out laughing. "Oh, inspector! It's obvious you've spent no time around politicians. The amount of two-faced pussy-footing that goes on, you wouldn't believe. Sweetness and light while they're talking to someone, and then, as soon as their back's turned, wham, in goes the knife." He caught his breath. "But don't take that as an admission that I know anything about what's happened to Mrs. Ronson, because I don't. Just a figure of speech. And as for the question of politicians not being honest and trying to cover up the truth, pardon me if I don't seem surprised. Big news! Politician tells lies! Hold the front page!"

Constable declined to be amused. "Can we move on to specifics please, sir? If you've heard something that's relevant, I need to know."

"Ask away."

Constable sighed inwardly. Information was not proving easy to extract. "Sergeant," he said sharply, turning to his junior colleague. "Remind me. I think you made a note of the seating arrangements down at the Dammett Well, didn't you?"

"Certainly did, sir."

"Look them up for me, would you?"

The sound of pages being leafed through. "Got it, sir."

"Tell me, who was seated alongside Mrs. Ronson at the dining table?"

"She had Mr. Grade on one side, and Mr. Stalker on the other, sir."

"Right. Thank you." Constable turned back to Jim. "So, Mr. Daly, did you hear any of the exchanges between Mrs. Ronson and either of the two gentlemen?"

"Not Milo Grade, no. The pub landlord and his girl were mostly looking after that end of the table."

"But Mr. Stalker? It sounds to me as if you did hear something there?"

"Well ..." Jim seemed disposed to tease the detectives. "Maybe there was something." He screwed his eyes up as if in recollection. "Oh, yes, that was it. There was talk about when he'd been on T.V., not too long back, and DiDo said something about him guarding his tongue, and he made some sort of snappy retort like 'Ah, but what if there aren't any guards?', or some such. She didn't seem at all amused by that, and she said something about what he'd said not being defensible, or there being no defence if he carried on like that. Something of the sort, anyway. I couldn't really hang about eavesdropping too obviously, although it sounded as if it could have been pretty interesting. But I saw the look in her eyes – it's no wonder he pulled his horns in a bit after that, and I don't think I heard much said between them afterwards."

"What about anyone else seated nearby?" asked Constable. "Sergeant, who was on the other side of the table?"

"That would be Miss Mayall, sir. Sorry, 'Ms' Mayall."

"Ah, the lovely Erica," said Jim. "Secretary of State for Women's Affairs." He laughed softly. "Don't you love irony in politics? Young, beautiful ... what's not to like?" The look on his face seemed to indicate a deeper meaning to his words.

"And Mrs. Ronson?" enquired Constable, striving to pick up on the hint in Jim's manner. "Are you telling me that, for some reason, she did not like Ms. Mayall?"

Jim gave him an odd look. "I don't think I said anything of the kind, inspector. As far as I can find out, they were very good friends. Of course, there's a shared history. I mean, they came into the House of Commons together, didn't they, so that makes for a close relationship, doesn't it? Although ..."

"Yes?"

"Although you might not have thought it

from one or two of the things that got said last night."

"And what might these have been, Mr. Daly?" Constable attempted to disguise his growing impatience at the way he seemed to be having to extract the information from his witness.

"Well, for some reason, DiDo seemed to have taken exception to Erica Mayall's shoes."

"What?"

"I know, inspector. Sounds daft, doesn't it? But I only know what I heard."

"Doesn't that tie in with something Mr. Stalker mentioned to us, sir?" put in Dave Copper.

"It might well do, sergeant, but I don't see the relevance. So what exactly did you hear, Mr. Daly?"

"DiDo said ..."

"I really don't approve of the way you speak of her, sir," interrupted Constable. "Could we have a little more respect for the dead woman?"

Jim raised his eyebrows. "Sorry about that, inspector. It's just my way of talking. Force of habit. No offence intended. So, anyway, the ... Prime Minister ... said something like 'I don't much care where you go to buy your shoes', and then she said 'No, actually, that's not true. And what people will care even more about is how you buy them. Or anything else'. And Erica retorted something about a duty to her constituency, and DiDo ... sorry, the P.M. said that anything Erica had been given could soon be taken away. It wasn't that easy to hear, because Perry Neal was blaring on to Lew Stalker something about the press, which I was also half-distracted by, and by then the two women were pretty much hissing at one another under their breaths. I would have loved to hear more, because if there's one thing I enjoy, it's a good cat-fight, but you can only take so long clearing a dinner plate, can't you?"

Constable paused for a moment to let the information sink in. "Anything else that strikes you, Mr. Daly? You seem to have quite a facility for remembering conversations."

"Comes in quite handy in my line of work, inspector."

"Sorry, sir. How do you mean?"

A slow smile crept across Jim's face. "When you're taking orders for meals and so on, inspector. That's all. It helps to cultivate a memory for what's said to you."

Constable couldn't help the feeling that he was being ribbed. "So, was anything else said to you? Or, at least, in your hearing? Wasn't anyone else seated at the end of the table where you were working?"

"Only Marion Hayste, inspector, and I don't think she contributed that much to the conversation at all. In fact, as far as I remember, she hardly uttered a peep during the whole meal, so I'm afraid I've got no beans to spill there. Sorry."

The inspector got to his feet abruptly. "In

that case, Mr. Daly, we'll call that it for the present. But if anything else occurs to you, I hope you'll let me know."

"I'll be sure to do so, inspector. But for now, I think I'll just take a little snooze." Jim settled back on the sofa and closed his eyes.

Exchanging glances with Dave Copper, Constable headed for the door, but paused with his hand on the handle. "Oh, just one thing, Mr. Daly," he said. "I'm just wondering how you came to be doing this job. You don't seem entirely the type."

"And what type would that be exactly, inspector?" challenged Jim, opening one eye. He sat back up. "Sure, there's no mystery to it. I fancied a bit of a career change, that's all," he explained airily. "I'd done a couple of spells of working in restaurants and bars during my student gap year, and I happened to know someone who knew someone who said there might be a vacancy in the catering staff at Downing Street. Turned out to be right – you wouldn't believe the turnover of people they have there. You know the saying – 'you can't get the staff'. And they were glad to have me. It's been interesting being close to the heart of things, so to speak. But who knows? With all this that's happened, I might move on now. Maybe it's all a little too exciting for an ordinary Irish boy. I might find better ways to spend my time." He gave a candid grin.

"Hmmm. Well, for the moment, don't move on too far," responded Constable. "I think we might want to speak to you again."

"Whenever you like, inspector. I'm not going to be sneaking off, am I? And who knows, I might want to have a long conversation with you at some point. Well, don't let me keep you." He settled back down again, eyes closed, the shadow of a grin remaining on his features.

*

"What do you make of all that, then, guv?" enquired Dave Copper, as the detectives stood in the centre of the hall.

"Which do you mean? The person or the evidence?" Andy Constable's face still wore a slight frown.

"Both, I suppose, sir."

"To be honest, I don't really know. He's told us some things which I'm sure are probably relevant, once we've had a chance to pick them apart, but I don't like the fact that our Mr. Daly seems to be enjoying himself far more than he ought to be. Not that I'm worried that he may have been responsible for Mrs. Ronson's death – we know for a fact that he couldn't have been involved in any way. But things I can't put my finger on have a tendency to bother me."

"So would it be a good idea to put him on the back burner for now, guv?" suggested Copper with a meaningful glance at his watch. "I mean, time's getting on, and you wanted to talk to Gideon Porter and his people down at the pub. All the more so, now that we know that the chat over dinner wasn't quite as chummy as some people have made out."

"My thoughts exactly, sergeant. Let's get straight to it." Constable headed for the front door, but was forestalled by the sound of footsteps on the staircase. He turned to see Sheila Deare descending the stairs. "Ah, Inspector Deare, just the person. I expect you'll be wanting an update. I've spoken to all your ministers, and Copper and I are just off down to the village now to interview some more potential witnesses. I hope we shan't be too long. In the meantime, I assume you'll continue to hold things together here."

"Oh, is that what I'm doing?" responded Sheila grimly. "It's not exactly an easy task. I've been round to all of them in your wake, and they seem to have regarded your enquiries as anything between an intrusion and an irrelevance. But they are getting increasingly fractious at being kept under house arrest, as one of them put it."

"And I'm afraid that, as things stand, that's the way things will have to remain," replied Constable firmly.

"Fortunately, with the passage of time," said Sheila with a ghost of a smile, "they're becoming more concerned about the state of their stomachs. Hunger pangs are beginning to kick in, and I've had enquiries about lunch, so I was just on my way down to see Mr. Knightly to see what he can arrange."

"Good idea." Constable nodded approvingly. "Give everybody something to occupy themselves with. But trays in the rooms again, please. And tell Mr. Knightly to attend to everything personally again. Keep Mr. Daly where he is – I don't want him wandering about the house unsupervised."

Sheila looked surprised. "You don't think that he ..."

"Not for a moment," Constable cut in. "But until I've satisfied myself about one or two things regarding Mr. Daly, we'll let him stay put."

Sheila shrugged. "Whatever you wish. It's your investigation. Well, I'll set the wheels in motion for the lunches." She moved towards the door leading to the kitchen corridor.

"And when we come back, there's something I want to ask you about," said Constable, continuing towards the front door. "But I think it will keep for now. We both have to get on." A thought struck him. "Oh, and while we're away, you may well get one of our other colleagues turning up here."

"Really? Who?"

"Sergeant Una Singleton from my SOCO team."

Sheila turned, annoyance plain on her features. "No, I'm sorry, I can't allow that, inspector. You know perfectly well what my instructions are, and that means they're your instructions as well. No further outsiders."

Constable stood firm. "Frankly, Ms. Deare, I don't give a damn. As you pointed out just now, this is my investigation, and nobody, not even the topmost of your top brass, is going to stop me carrying it out the best way I know how. And Una

Singleton is not exactly an outsider – she is a very talented officer and extremely discreet. My sergeant here can vouch for that, can't you, Copper?"

"Er ... that's right, sir. I told her what you said. She says no problem."

"So, if you'll give her every courtesy, inspector, I shall be grateful," said Constable with finality. "And now, if you will excuse us, we are off to the pub." The front door closed behind the detectives.

Chapter 8

The Dammett Well Inn stood, as it had done for many centuries, as a prominent feature of the High Street of Dammett Worthy. A long low timber-framed building, its traditional black-and-white frontage was enlivened with a profusion of hanging baskets which provided bright multi-coloured splashes of foliage and flowers. The Inspector drew his car to a halt at the edge of the village green next to the church, and the two police officers climbed out and surveyed the scene.

"Not changed a lot, has it guv?" remarked Dave Copper.

"Since the last time we were here?" replied Andy Constable. "No, I don't suppose it has, in appearance. Although I don't think you'd really expect it to. Life in these English country villages tends to move at a rather less frenetic pace than we're used to in town. I don't think they're necessarily too fond of a great deal of excitement."

"Seems to me they're getting more than their fair share, in that case, guv," said Copper with a grin. "What with the business last time at the fête, and now all this with the Prime Minister, this place probably doesn't qualify as a typical English village any more."

Constable smiled faintly. "And actually, the closer you look, the more you notice. For example, look at the sign outside the tea-rooms down there. That's not called 'The Copper Kettle' any more. And I'd be surprised if there hadn't been some changes at the solicitors' offices. And, of course, with the Hall itself changing hands, I wouldn't be astonished if there have been more alterations to life around here than are visible on the surface."

"I wonder who's living in Horace Cope's cottage these days," mused Copper.

"Fortunately," said Constable briskly, "we don't have to trouble ourselves with pointless speculation about irrelevancies. Let's get on with the job in hand." He crossed the road to the Dammett Well Inn and pushed open the door of the saloon bar.

"Blow me down!" came the instant greeting, in tones of cheery surprise. "If it ain't Mr. Constable! And Sergeant Copper too, if I ain't mistook. Well, it's been a fair old while since I saw you two gents." An arm was extended across the bar, and vigorous handshakes were exchanged.

Gideon Porter provided a reassuringly familiar presence, whatever changes might have been taking place in the village around him. The round face of the Dammett Well's landlord was perhaps a little redder than when the detectives had first encountered him, the head a little balder, the spectacular mutton-chop whiskers a little more sprinkled with grey, but there was no change to the robust welcoming demeanour and ringing country burr which had been extending the hospitality of his house to his customers for longer than most people could remember.

"What'll it be then, gentlemen?" enquired Gideon. "I hope you've got time for a little drop of something, on the house, and we can have a bit of a chin-wag about that time you were here before. Did me no end of good, that business did, what with all the extra custom I got from people turning up to see where it all happened after the case was in all the papers. Ghouls, some people, I know, but it's an ill wind, as they say. So, what's your pleasure?"

"No pleasure at all, I'm afraid, Mr. Porter," replied Constable. "Unfortunately it's business once again."

Gideon's face fell. "Oh, don't tell me. Don't say they've gone and found someone else dead."

"That's exactly what has happened, Mr. Porter," said Constable. "And you were so helpful to us last time that I'm hoping you'll be able to do the same again this time. Particularly given the circumstances."

"Why, who's dead? It's not one of my customers, is it?"

"Not exactly, Mr. Porter. Look, is there somewhere we can have a discreet talk? The bar of a pub isn't the most private place for what we have to discuss."

"Well, I'm not exactly run off my feet with customers at the moment, inspector, as you can see, so we should be all right here. Tell you what, we'll go round the corner into the old snug, and then we won't be overheard, even if someone does come in. Hold on just a sec." Gideon turned, opened a door at the back of the bar, and bellowed 'Jerry!' in stentorian tones. After a few moments, a virtual carbon copy of the landlord, some thirty-five years younger and with flaming red hair but with the same sturdy build and ruddy face, appeared in the doorway. "Jerry, take over the bar for me for a bit, would you? I've got to go and have a word with these two gentlemen."

"Okay, dad, will do."

"My oldest, Jeremiah," explained Gideon over his shoulder, as he led the detectives round the corner to a comfortable seating area next to an inglenook fireplace. "He's my chef. A good one, too." The three settled themselves, and Gideon gave an enquiring look.

"So, inspector, what's up?"

Constable drew a long breath. "Mr. Porter, what I'm about to tell you has to be treated in the strictest confidence."

Gideon chuckled. "Oh, that's one thing you don't have to worry about with me, inspector. I know how to keep my mouth shut. I tell you, some of the things I get to hear across the bar don't bear repeating." He tapped his forehead. "I got more secrets tucked away in my noggin than you could shake a stick at. In fact, you might say that, round here, I pretty much know where all the bodies are buried." He gave a broad smile, which slowly faded at the inspector's unwavering countenance. "Sorry. I s'pose, after that business up at the Hall fête, that ain't a very tasteful thing to say. But why all the long faces now? 'Ere, that old case ain't reared its ugly head again, has it?"

"Not exactly, Mr. Porter. No, on this occasion, it's the Prime Minister."

"She ain't complained, has she?" said Gideon in worried tones. "'Cos she seemed such a nice woman when we was talking last night when she got here, and I thought it all went pretty well, and she seemed quite happy when they left. Why, what's she said to you?"

"Nothing at all, unfortunately. She hasn't exactly been in a position to do so, I'm afraid. In fact, I'm sorry to have to tell you that it's Mrs. Ronson who is dead."

"What?" Gideon was aghast. "Oh, don't tell me it's food poisoning. No, it couldn't be, 'cos everyone had the same last night. Unless they've all come down with it. They haven't, have they? No, they can't have, because there was food left over after we'd served all the meals, and my people and me, we all finished it off for our supper, and we're all okay. See, it was a Caesar salad to start off with, 'cos that's pretty simple and it don't take a lot of fiddling about to serve, and then we done them a Moroccan lamb tadjine, and that's all done in the one big pot, and there was couscous to go with that, and after that it was fruit, so I don't see how ..."

With no little difficulty, Constable succeeded in stemming Gideon's increasingly panicky babble. "Mr. Porter ... Mr. Porter ... slow down." Against his will, he gave a hint of a smile. "You don't have to worry about the reputation of your kitchen, or your son. There was nothing at all wrong with the food you served. As far as I'm aware, everyone is in the best of health."

"Except Mrs. Ronson, of course, guv," remarked Copper under his breath.

"Yes, thank you, sergeant." Constable rounded on his junior with some asperity. "I'm not at all sure that levity is going to serve us best in this situation."

"No, sir. Sorry, sir." Copper dipped his head into his notebook and prepared to take notes.

"So, inspector, what has happened?" enquired Gideon. He caught his breath. "'Ere, it's not another murder, is it?"

"I'm afraid that's exactly what it is, Mr. Porter."

Gideon slumped. "'Course it is. That's why you two gents are here. Couldn't be anything else, I reckon. Who'd have thought it? Our little village in the middle of a murder case. Again." He sighed deeply, but then straightened and visibly appeared to pull himself together. "So, inspector, how can I help? You obviously ain't here on a social call."

"Very much not, Mr. Porter. The fact that the Prime Minister and her colleagues were dining here last night is quite possibly very relevant to our investigations."

"How's that, then?"

"You told us yourself, sir. I understand from Mrs. Ronson's security officer that you and a couple of other people were engaged in serving the meal. That would have given you an opportunity to hear anything that may have been said between those present which might give us an inkling as to who could have had some sort of motivation to harm the Prime Minister." Constable grimaced at all the convoluted conditionals. "So, my question is, did you or any of the other staff hear anything of the sort?"

"You'll have to ask them about that, inspector. I can only answer for meself."

"We have already spoken to the waiter who came with the government party, Mr. Porter. He's told us a few very interesting things. Now I'm hoping you can add to them." Constable leaned forward expectantly. "So please ... can you help me out?"

Gideon puffed his cheeks out. "I don't know as I can, Mr. Constable. I was mostly concerned with making sure that everything got served properly. See, you got to admit, it was a bit intimidating, having the Prime Minister and half the Cabinet sat round the table."

"Yes, I can see that," agreed Constable. "But you said Mrs. Ronson seemed a nice woman when she arrived, and if I've been informed correctly, I think you were serving her yourself for at least some of the time. So surely," he coaxed, "you would have caught something of the conversation."

"Well, maybe. But far as I can recall, it was mostly about nothing much."

"No hasty words?" persisted the inspector. "No hints of any differences of opinion."

Gideon furrowed his brow. "'Ere, hang on.

You might be on to something there. You just reminded me of something."

"And that would be ...?"

"Well, it was all a bit funny, really. It was when we were serving up the main course – you know, that Moroccan lamb thing. And in fact, I wasn't by Mrs. Ronson at all – I was over the other side of the table serving one of the other ladies ... Mandy something ... she's the Foreign Secretary, I think ..."

"Miss Laye? Amanda Laye?"

"That's the one, inspector," nodded Gideon. "Anyway, I was giving her her food, and she said it smelled good and she asked what it was, so I told her, and then Mrs. Ronson must have overheard, because she leaned across and said 'I'm surprised you didn't recognise it, Mandy. I'd have thought you'd be pretty familiar with all things Middle Eastern', and then Miss Laye gave a sort of mumble and a smile, and Mrs. Ronson went on saying something about her 'having acquired a taste for Arab food, and quite a lot of other things, back when she was a student'. Shame she didn't study law like Mrs. Nye while she was at it, she said. And Miss Laye was starting to look a bit pink, and she said she didn't know what the Prime Minister was getting at, and Mrs. Ronson said something about it being no big deal, no need to get up in arms about it, or something of the sort. But then I got on with serving other people, so I don't know if it went any further."

Constable paused for a moment in

consideration. "Hmmm. On the face of it, you wouldn't think an exchange of words over the contents of a dinner plate ought to be major cause for concern. But you never know. I'll give it some thought."

"Chew it over later, eh, guv?" suggested Copper brightly, but then subsided under his superior's stony gaze.

"So was there anything else that caught your ear, Mr. Porter?" said Constable, turning back to the publican. "Anything out of kilter with ordinary social conversation?"

"Not at the table, inspector, no, but there was something afterwards, when everybody was leaving."

"Oh yes? And what was that?"

"Well, they were starting to get into their cars, and I was holding the car door for Mrs. Ronson and saying goodbye, and she was saying how much she'd enjoyed the meal, one way and another, and then one of the other ministers was just going past, you know, to get into the other car, 'cos they'd only come in just the two, which seemed to me to be a bit of a squash, what with them all being important people, cabinet ministers and suchlike ..." Gideon broke off, conscious of having lost his train of thought. "Now, where was I?"

"Holding the car door, sir," prompted Copper, looking up from his notes.

"That's right. And Mrs. Ronson was speaking to me, but then she broke off as one of the chaps went by, and said 'Oh, Benny'..."

"That would be Benjamin Fitt, I assume?"

"If you say so, inspector. I don't follow all the ins and outs of politics. These days, it's all too confusing."

"So what did Mrs. Ronson have to say to Mr. Fitt, sir?"

"She said as how she'd had a very interesting conversation with his P.P.S., whatever that may be ..."

"I think you'll find that's Parliamentary Private Secretary, Mr. Porter. It means an M.P. who is a sort of unpaid assistant to a minister."

"Well, you'd know that better than me, inspector. Anyway, she said something about it being a funny coincidence that Mr. Fitt had chosen, as this P.P.S. thing of his, the M.P. for the constituency where Mr. Fitt hisself grew up. And Mr. Fitt gave a sort of half-laugh and said you did get some funny old coincidences in politics, and then Mrs. Ronson said something about 'not many coincidences as funny as the name of one of the ladies who'd gone to this M.P. for help'. But then she said there'd be plenty of time to talk about that back up at the Hall, and then she climbed into the car, and off they all went."

Constable glanced at his junior. "Got all that, Copper?"

"I think so, sir," replied the sergeant, flexing his wrist. "Although I really wish I'd learnt shorthand. I think I'm going to record stuff on my phone in future."

"Sorry about that, sergeant," said Gideon. "I know I go on a bit, but I reckon that's probably everything I can tell you, 'cos they all went off in their cars straight after that, so you can give your fingers a bit of a rest."

"Ah, sadly he can't, Mr. Porter," contradicted Constable. "You weren't the only person serving last night, were you? And that being the case, we're going to have to speak to your waitress as well. If you can tell me where she lives. Is she a local girl?"

"She is, inspector. She lives at Cross's Farm, just round the corner and up Sloe Lane, but you don't need to go chasing after her. She's here. She helps out my Jerry in the kitchen, doing veg prep and suchlike. She's out there now."

"That's extremely convenient, sir."

Gideon heaved himself to his feet. "Do you want me to go and get her?"

"Would you, please, Mr. Porter." Constable halted the landlord as he moved towards the kitchen. "But I think it would be best if you didn't tell her why we're here. I'm under strict instructions to keep this whole case under wraps as long as possible, given all its ramifications. In fact, I probably shouldn't have told you, except that I know I can rely on your discretion."

"I don't need telling twice, inspector," said Gideon solemnly. "You leave it to me. I'll just say that something's come up after last night's meal, and you'd like to ask her a few questions. How's that?"

"That would do perfectly, Mr. Porter."

With a nod, Gideon turned and headed for the bar, and a few moments later, a young girl appeared around the corner of the snug. She looked to be approaching twenty, slightly plump, with fair hair and a fresh country complexion. She hesitated when she saw the detectives.

"Gideon says you want to see me," she faltered.

"Oh, nothing to worry about." Constable sought to put the girl at ease by assuming his most comfortable and avuncular manner. "We're police officers." He introduced himself and his colleague. "It's just that we need to ask you a few questions about what happened at the dinner here last night, because there's a matter we're looking into, and we hope you might have heard something that could help us. So why don't you sit down, and we'll have a little chat."

The girl perched on the edge of a chair, still looking apprehensive.

"Can I just make a note of your name, miss," said Copper gently, taking his cue from his superior officer.

"Yes. It's Lena."

"Would that be short for anything?"

Lena blushed. "Do I have to tell you?"

"If you wouldn't mind, miss," persisted Copper with a puzzled look. "Just so's I've got everything correct. So, Lena is short for ... what? Angelina, is it?"

Lena gave a profound sigh. "Please, don't tell anyone. It's so embarrassing." She took a deep breath, and then blurted, "It's Thumbelina."

Copper maintained an admirably straight face. "Oh yes, miss." He swallowed. "That's ... er

... unusual."

Lena looked thoroughly downcast. "It's my mum's fault. She always loved that fairy story when she was a kid, and after she'd seen that film about Hans Christian Andersen, that was it. My gran says she never stopped singing the song. So when I was born, she stuck me with the name. My dad never got a word in. But you won't let on, will you?" she pleaded. "I'd never hear the last of it from my friends."

"Your secret is safe with us, miss," Copper assured her. "And can I just make a note of the surname?" He mentally crossed his fingers that there were to be no more unconventional revelations forthcoming.

"It's Cross."

"Thank you, miss. And I gather that you live in the village. Oh, of course, it's at Cross's Farm, isn't it?"

"Yes. It's my dad's farm. We keep cattle."

Constable took over the interview. "But you work here for Mr. Porter. How long have you been doing that?"

"Since I left school. A bit more than a year now."

"Not tempted to go into the family business?" smiled Constable.

"I'm not really that fond of cows," replied Lena with a moue. "They stand on your feet."

"So you came here to work at the Dammett Well, helping out Mr. Porter and his son," said Constable, gently bringing the conversation around to the investigation. "And you were one of those who served the meal to the private party who dined here last night."

"Yes." Lena gave a slight giggle. "Actually, it was pretty scary. I mean, Gideon had told me I'd be needed to serve a private party in the dining room, but he didn't say anything more than that, so when the Prime Minister and all these other important people turned up, I got really nervous in case I did something stupid like spilling the food down someone."

"So you knew who the guests were?"

"Well, not really. I knew Mrs. Ronson, of course, because I'd seen her on the telly, and I think I'd seen some of the other faces, but I didn't know their names. Why, is it important?"

"No, not in the least, miss." Constable gave an inward sigh. This was not going to make the task of gathering information any easier. "But what I'd like to ask is, if by any chance you heard any of the conversations between the ministers during the course of your duties."

"I don't really know. I wasn't paying that much attention ..." Lena frowned in thought, but then her face cleared. "Oh, there was one thing. And I wouldn't have listened, except that someone was talking about school exam results and whether they were getting better or worse. I didn't do very well in my exams when I left school," she confessed with a touch of embarrassment. "But one of the gentlemen ... I think he was the one sitting on Mrs. Ronson's right ..."

"Hold on a second, miss," intervened

Copper. He leafed swiftly through the pages of his notebook. "I think that would have been Mr. Grade, sir."

"Sounds likely," agreed Constable. "So what were they saying, Lena?"

"It was something about whether the figures were being fiddled, and the gentleman said he was going to crack down on anything of the sort, and Mrs. Ronson sort of sneered and asked who was going to check up on the people doing the checks. She said something about a qualified opinion. And then the lady sat the other side of the gentleman, she said some foreign expression ... something like 'quis' ... 'quis' ... no, I can't remember what it was."

"'*Quis custodiet ipsos custodes*?', perhaps?" suggested Constable. And in response to Lena's shrug, "'Who guards the guards?'" he explained. "So that lady would have been ...?" He turned to Copper for verification.

"Mrs. Nye, sir."

"Thought as much. It's the sort of legal Latin you'd hope the Justice Secretary would have at her fingertips. Anyway, do go on, Lena. Did they say any more?"

"Well, Mrs. Ronson said something about there being fraud everywhere you turned, it seemed to her. And nobody's family was exempt, specially those with the highest connections. Parents, wives, husbands. 'But you'd know that better than me, Dee, wouldn't you?', she said. But everything had to come out into the open in the end."

"She didn't get more specific?"

"No, and I didn't hear any more, because Gideon came up and gave me a nudge because he thought I was being slow, so I had to come back to the kitchen."

Constable paused for a moment to digest the waitress's statements. "I see. And did you have a chance to hear any of the other guests talking between themselves during the meal?"

"Well no, not really. See, when I was back in the kitchen, Gideon told me off because he thought I'd been eavesdropping on purpose, which I wasn't, so I made sure I got on with things after that and didn't hang about. Anyway, once they got to the coffee, I didn't go back into the dining room any more, because Gideon wanted me to help Jerry with the clearing up in the kitchen, so I stayed out there after that." She twisted her fingers together in her lap. "In fact, I ought to get back out there, or else Jerry'll be after me if everything's not ready in time for him to do the lunches."

"Of course, Lena," said Constable with an easy smile. "If you've told us all you know, then we won't keep you. You must get back to your work."

Lena stood. "I'm sorry. It doesn't sound as if I know very much. I mean, about whatever it is you wanted. I don't suppose I've helped at all, have I?"

"I'm sure you have," Constable reassured her. "Don't give it another thought. Off you go now."

"And you won't say anything about ... you know?" With a shaky smile and a nervous backward glance, Lena made her escape.

Chapter 9

Gideon Porter had resumed his normal place behind the bar, and was engaged in polishing glasses as the detectives made their way back into the main room of the Dammett Well Inn.

"'Ere, I hope you ain't been upsetting my staff, inspector," he said, looking up. "'Cos Lena, she's just shot off into the back like a startled ferret."

"I hope we haven't done anything of the sort, Mr. Porter," replied Andy Constable. "We always try to be as un-intimidating as possible, except when it comes down to the really hardened villains, and I can't really see that your Miss Cross comes into that category. But when you see her, do please reassure her that whatever she's told us is in complete confidence, and she doesn't need to worry about it going any further."

"Ah. Well, that's all right then. She's a good girl. And I hope whatever she had to say was useful."

"That remains to be seen, Mr. Porter. We shall have to give some thought to everything we've been told. In the meantime, Copper and I should be getting along."

Gideon looked around and lowered his voice, as if expecting eavesdroppers to be lurking in the corners of the bar. "So do you reckon you're any closer to finding out who did this to

Mrs. ... you know who?"

Constable gave a slight grimace. "Who can tell? But at least we've covered what she did when she was here in the village."

"Well, some of it, anyway," said Gideon.

Constable's attention was alerted. "Sorry, Mr. Porter? How do you mean?"

"Well, I'd seen her earlier, of course, hadn't I?" stated the publican.

"Really?" Constable was torn between surprise and exasperation. "And you didn't think to mention this?"

"I didn't think of it till now," responded Gideon defensively. "Over to the church, it was. Only caught a glimpse, mind, but it was her all right. Getting out of that big black car of hers. It was the car I noticed first. Parked behind the other one. And I thought, 'Who's that, then?', and then of course I realised. But she didn't come over here, so I never spoke to her then. No, she headed off towards the church."

"So you can't tell us any more?"

"No. Maybe you'd be better off having a word with the vicar."

"Oh yes." Constable smiled in fond recollection. "I remember Mr. Pugh very well. Charming old chap."

"Oh no," said Gideon. "No, he ain't with us any more. He went ... oh, must be about two year ago."

"Oh. Where did he go?" enquired Copper. "Wasn't he a bit old to go off to another parish?"

"He went to join the choir invisible,

sergeant," explained the landlord. "And now he's taking his eternal rest in the churchyard, along of his parishioners."

"Ah. Sorry," said Copper humbly.

"So if it's anything about the church you're after, inspector, you'd best have a word with Rory."

"Rory?"

"The new vicar."

"And where will I find him?"

Gideon chuckled. "Just through in the other bar, inspector. Popped in for a chat and a swift half just before you arrived." He raised his voice. "Rory ... if you ain't busy, can you pop through for a word?"

The door to the lounge bar opened, and a woman appeared. She was plump and cheerful-looking, with dark brown hair worn in a chin-length bob, and her age was difficult to guess - somewhere around forty, estimated Constable. And the bright purple cardigan she was draped in almost, but not quite, drew attention away from the clerical collar she wore. In her hand were the dregs of a glass of stout. She advanced on the detectives with a broad smile.

"Good morning, gentlemen." She extended a hand towards Constable. "Rory English. What can I do for you?"

"Rory?" queried Copper, pen poised above his notebook.

"Short for Aurora," explained the vicar. "Roman Goddess of the Dawn. Although I've never thought of myself as particularly goddess-like. As you can see." She laughed, indicating her generous frame. "And anyway, I wouldn't want to seem disrespectful to my ultimate boss. So please, just call me Rory."

"And this is Inspector Constable and Sergeant Copper," introduced Gideon.

"I thought I detected the whiff of officialdom," said Rory. "So, how can I help?"

"They've had trouble up at the Hall ..." began Gideon.

"I think, perhaps," Constable forestalled him, "that we'd better take it from here, Mr. Porter. In the interests of discretion." He gave the landlord a warning look.

"Ah. Right you are, inspector." Gideon winked. "My lips is sealed. Publican's honour."

Rory drained the remnants of her glass. "Look, I was just on my way back over to the church, inspector. Why don't you walk with me, and you can tell me what this is all about."

"By all means." Constable held back the door, and the three emerged on to the High Street and headed towards the church.

The Parish Church of St. Salyve was a typical example of the ancient places of worship found in so many English country villages. Built in the local mellow grey stone with scattered adornments of flint-work, it sat comfortably at the heart of a picturesque churchyard dotted with moss-grown tombstones, many of them tilted to a rakish angle, interspersed with the severe classical table-tombs of worthies from the eighteenth century and the more extravagant statuary-adorned monuments of their Victorian descendants. Noble horse-chestnut trees, their splay-fingered leaves rustling in the gentle breeze, seemed to defer to a venerable yew, many of whose aged limbs required the aid of timber supports.

As the three passed through the lychgate, Constable was moved to remark, "This is a very fine church you have here, reverend."

"Rory, please," replied the vicar. "I like to run the parish as informally as I can. Lord knows, we have to do something these days to avoid scaring people away." She smiled comfortably. "But yes, you're right, inspector. It's a lovely building. I feel very lucky to have been posted here."

"Norman, isn't it?"

"Mostly, yes. The tower's got a bit of Saxon in it, and there's some rather surprising fan-vaulting in the Lady Chapel. Actually, we were very lucky. The Victorians almost got their hands on the building and started carrying out some of their pseudo-medieval so-called improvements, but fortunately, the diocese ran out of money at just the right time, so they only got as far as adding a rather snooty Gothic side-aisle on the far side of the church. You can't see it from here."

"Something of a blessing, I gather."

"You might very well say that, inspector," smiled Rory. She shot a sideways look at Constable. "However, I dare say you haven't come here to discuss ecclesiastical architecture. So you'd better come inside, we can make ourselves comfortable in the vestry, and you can tell me what this is all about." She held open the massive iron-bound oaken door, obviously a veteran of many centuries of use, and ushered the detectives into the cool interior, where dust-motes twinkled in the sunbeams falling from the stained-glass windows.

"Take a seat, gentlemen," said the vicar as she led the way into the vestry, indicating a pair of battered cane garden chairs facing her desk. "I dare say I could rustle up a cup of tea, if you have the time. Isn't that what one is always supposed to offer the police when they come calling?"

"Time presses, I'm afraid, vic... Rory," replied Constable.

"In that case, inspector," said Rory, settling herself into the well-worn captain's chair behind her desk, "you'd better tell me what brings you here."

"A case of murder, I'm afraid, vicar," said Constable bluntly.

"In the village?" Rory sounded shocked. "Oh, that's dreadful. Can I ask who? Is it one of my parishioners?"

"It's even more serious that that," responded Constable. "The murder took place up at Dammett Hall last night, and the victim is Mrs. Ronson, the Prime Minister."

Rory gazed in astonishment at the detectives, her hand half-way to her mouth. Horror was written across her face. "Oh inspector. How appalling. But I was speaking to her only yesterday ..." She tailed off, swallowed, and blinked rapidly two or three times. "Excuse me just a moment." She closed her eyes, and her lips moved silently in prayer. After a few seconds, she took a deep breath and raised her head. "So, Mr. Constable, how can I help?"

"I understand from Gideon Porter," began Constable, "that Mrs. Ronson was seen coming into the church yesterday afternoon."

"That's right," nodded Rory. "In fact, she was the second of my visitors."

"Really?"

"Mr. Porter did mention that Mrs. Ronson's car was parked behind another one, sir," pointed out Dave Copper.

"So he did, sergeant. Thank you."

"That's correct," said Rory. "I was out at the lychgate, pinning up a notice on the parish noticeboard, when the car drew up. It was one of those large black important-looking ones, and I thought, 'Who's this?', and then out of the car stepped the minister."

"A government minister, are you saying?"

"Good Lord, yes," chuckled Rory. "Church of England ministers don't get to ride in anything so impressive, and especially not if it's chauffeur-driven. Well, unless it's one of the grander bishops, but even they are having to pull their horns in somewhat in these days of austerity. Anyway, I digress."

"So, this minister. Did you recognise who it was?"

"Actually, yes, because I'd seen him on television not long ago. I told him so – we don't get that many public figures visiting us. There was a programme that caught my eye about the hospice movement versus assisted dying, and he was interviewed on that."

"And it was ...?"

"Dr. Neal. He's the Health Secretary, isn't he?"

"He is indeed, vicar. So what brought him to your church, I wonder?"

"He just said that it had caught his eye when passing, and he thought he might come in and have a look around. Lots of people do – there's nothing really surprising about it. And as I didn't have anything more pressing to do at the time, I offered to give him the guided tour. Some of the stained glass is quite a rare survival from the middle ages, and some people think our font could well be the Saxon original. It's certainly battered enough. And the Lawdown monument is very impressive – it's still got all its seventeenth century original colouring, and everybody seems to be quite intrigued by the line-up of six sons and seven daughters along the bottom of the tomb. They'd all pre-deceased their parents, you see, and the wife had died shortly after the last one was born. Mr. Neal seemed quite touched when I told him the story. He's a widower, I believe." A solemn look came over Rory's face. "Sadly, so many of the associations of a building like this are to do with death. But it never becomes matter-of-fact."

"And did Dr. Neal enjoy his tour?"

Rory considered for a moment. "I don't

know that enjoyed is the right word. Moved, perhaps. Because when we'd finished, he asked if he could have a few minutes alone. I said of course, and I came back in here to give him some privacy, and the last I saw of him, he was walking up the nave towards the altar."

"So you didn't see him after that?"

"See, no. But I heard the door go a few minutes after that, and I thought it must be him leaving, but then I heard him speaking to someone who'd just come in. Which, of course, I now know to have been Mrs. Ronson, although I didn't realise that at the time. And I was just about to go out to see who it was, but then I caught a few words of the conversation, and it didn't really sound as if it would have been appropriate for me to intrude."

"And why would that be, vicar?" enquired Constable. "What were they speaking about?"

Rory hesitated. "This is awkward, inspector. I really don't know that I ought to repeat a private conversation overheard in my church."

"I quite see your point, vicar ... Rory." Constable smiled understandingly. "And if the circumstances were any different, I might well agree with you. But this is a murder investigation. I don't always have the luxury of observing all the niceties. Besides," he coaxed, "it's not as if you would be betraying the confidences of the confessional."

"You're thinking of my Catholic counterpart at the other end of the village," said Rory with a faint smile. She sighed. "But you're absolutely right. And you never know, what they said may be relevant."

"So what was it exactly?"

"They were talking about death, inspector."

Constable was somewhat taken aback. "How ...? I mean, whose ...?"

"It was all rather uncomfortable to listen to," continued Rory. "It was obvious that Mrs. Ronson had found Dr. Neal in the midst of praying, because I heard her say 'What's this, Perry? On your knees seeking forgiveness for your sins?'. And there was a bit of a scrambling noise, which must have been him getting to his feet in a hurry, and then he answered 'Well, haven't we all got plenty of those, Prime Minister?'. I think he tried to laugh the remark off, but she said something about not all of them leading to people dying. And then I imagine she must have been looking around at the various memorials dotted about on the walls, because she made a comment about everything ending in death."

"But this is not so very far from what you and Dr. Neal had been speaking about when you'd been showing him around," observed Constable.

"No," said Rory, "but then it got a little more pointed. He mumbled something, which I didn't catch, and then I could hear footsteps, which must have been Mrs. Ronson walking over to the Lawdown tomb. Because she said 'Here's a sad case. All these young lives, and a child and its mother in one fell swoop. Medical incompetence? Who can tell? In those days, doctors could get away with their mistakes. Things could be passed off as natural causes or covered up. Even up until quite recently, in fact. But not any more'."

"And what did Dr. Neal have to say to that?"

"He stammered something about the work of his department, and about how they were all committed to making sure that things like that could never happen. And she said that, when they did, they had to be rooted out. But she said there would be plenty of time to go into that later. I think he must have taken that as his cue to escape, because I heard him walking up the nave, and then the door slammed after that."

"So was there anything else?"

"No, not really. I left it for a few moments, and then I went out into the church, to find Mrs. Ronson just standing looking at the Lawdown tomb. I introduced myself, and we had a brief chat about nothing in particular. She mentioned that she was going to be up at the Hall for a meeting with some colleagues, but she didn't go into any detail. So I pointed out some of the things of interest around the church, but she seemed slightly distracted, and she left not long after that."

"She didn't refer to her conversation with Dr. Neal?"

"No, and I didn't think it was my place to bring it up, especially as it was obviously something that was never intended for other ears. I did ask if she might be joining us for the service on Sunday morning, but she said that she would be long gone by then." Rory closed her eyes at the realisation of the import of what she had said. "Strangely prophetic words, inspector."

"Indeed," said Constable. "Which would appear to close the matter as far as you are concerned."

"Not quite, Mr. Constable. Any death in my parish gives me cause for concern. I have my responsibilities to all the souls in my care, whether permanently or temporarily. So if there's nothing more I can tell you, I think I need to go and have a few words with someone else." Rory stood.

"Sorry, I don't quite ..." Constable caught on. "Ah. I see. Of course. Well, we shall leave you in peace to ... er ..." He nodded an indication to Copper and, after brief farewell handshakes, the two detectives made their way towards the porch. As they reached the door, Constable glanced back, to see Rory settling herself on her knees at the altar rail.

*

As the police officers emerged into the sunlight of the churchyard, the breeze, which had freshened considerably, was blowing a flurry of tattered old newspaper pages around and amongst the gravestones.

"See if you can grab those, sergeant," said Andy Constable. "The vicar's probably got quite enough to do without having to go round picking up litter."

Dave Copper obligingly scampered after the offending sheets, and eventually succeeded in gathering them up in an untidy bundle, together with half a dozen crisp packets, two beer cans, and an almost-deflated balloon bearing the legend 'Happy 7th Birthday'. He returned, puffing slightly, to his waiting superior and began to stuff his collection into the waste-bin alongside the lychgate, when something caught his eye. "Hold on a second, guv. Wow! Take a look at this."

"And this would be ...?"

"It's an old copy of the 'Daily Globe', sir. From some time last month. It's a bit soggy, but look here." He pointed to an article, somewhat mud-obscured, on one of the pages.

"And what is so interesting about 'The Daly Report'?" enquired Constable. "Apart from the dodgy spelling. I didn't think you were that bothered about current affairs."

"Never mind about the spelling, guv," retorted Copper. "Look at the picture." The headline of the article was accompanied by a thumbnail photograph of the author. "It's him."

"Him who?" The inspector studied the crumpled paper more closely. The caption to the grainy photograph left no room for uncertainty. Smiling from the page were the newly-familiar features of Seamus Daly.

Constable let out a sound somewhere between a sigh and a growl. He took the paper from his junior and gazed for a moment into the smudged newsprint eyes. "So that's who he is. I knew there was something about him that didn't seem right, but I was damned if I could put my finger on it." A thought struck him. "And that's what that note I found in the P.M.'s briefcase was about!"

"Sorry, guv? What note's that?"

"I didn't show it to you at the time, because you were busy finding notes of your own. But there was a piece of paper with a cryptic message on it, saying 'Not everyone is what they appear to be. S.D?'. I thought the S.D. was a signature from Sheila Deare. I was planning to ask her about it when we got back to the Hall. But it was nothing of the sort. I should have paid attention to the question mark. It was a note from somebody warning Mrs. Ronson that Seamus Daly was an impostor. So I'm looking forward to my next conversation with that gentleman. He's no more a waiter than I am. He's been planted by his newspaper to try to get some sort of inside story. The man's a tabloid journalist!"

Chapter 10

Andy Constable pulled in at the foot of the steps to the front door of Dammett Hall, alongside a small white hatchback whose tailgate bore the somewhat perplexing legend 'Powered by fairy dust'.

"She's here, then," observed Dave Copper. And at Constable's raised interrogative eyebrow, "Una, sir. Um ... Sergeant Singleton, I mean. And she obviously took on board what you said about discretion, sir," he hurried on, blushing slightly. "She's come in her own car instead of the official wagon."

"Very thoughtful of her," remarked Constable, attempting to stifle a smile. "You and I must have a little chat about discretion at some time. But in the meantime ... 'Powered by fairy dust'? What on earth is that all about?"

"Oh, it's just a little joke they have in the SOCO department. Something about magicking solid evidence out of virtually nothing."

"Most amusing, sergeant. Let's hope she's found a great deal more than nothing here. Shall we go and find out?" Constable led the way into the hall, to find Phil Knightly seated at the ornate Boule reception desk, rummaging through its drawers.

The hotel manager looked up as the detectives entered. "Oh, inspector, it's you. I hope you don't mind, but I'm trying to do some detecting of my own. So far I'm having precious little luck in solving my mystery."

"And what mystery would that be, sir?"

"I can't find the hotel register. It ought to be here, but there's no sign of it. I had the thought that I ought to get in touch with people who've made reservations to let them know that they won't be able to come, at least until you've given me the all-clear. I've got a list of all the reservations on the computer, of course, but I wanted the register to check whether any of them had been our guests before. People like the personal touch, you know. They're always impressed if you can say 'I hope you enjoyed yourselves when you were here last June', or whatever. And the register normally lives here on the desk, but it seems to have vanished."

"In that case," said Constable, "let me set your mind at rest. There's no mystery at all. The register is up in Mrs. Ronson's room. I noticed it there when we were conducting a search."

Phil looked puzzled. "Well, that's another mystery, inspector. What on earth was it doing up there?"

"That I'm afraid I can't answer, Mr. Knightly. But on the assumption that she had it for a reason, I don't think I can let you have it back until we've had a chance to take a look through it, just in case there's something instructive to be found. So I'm afraid you'll have to manage as best you can." He thought for a moment. "I think it's not unreasonable to allow you to call these guests of yours, but obviously I have to insist that you be discreet about the reason for the cancellation. Do you think you could devise some excuse involving the plumbing or the electrics, perhaps?"

Phil sighed. "I'll do my best, inspector. I should have had enough experience soothing ruffled feathers by now." He stood. "Well, I'd best get on with it. I'll be in my office if anyone wants me. Oh, by the way, someone from your squad, or whatever it is, arrived not long ago. Miss Singleton. She said she was here on your instructions. Inspector Deare has taken her through to the library."

"Thank you, Mr. Knightly. We'll check up on them now." Constable watched as Phil disappeared through the disguised door into his office, and then led the way into the library, where he found an overall-clad Una Singleton kneeling alongside the body of Doris Ronson, a case of equipment at her side, watched over by a tight-lipped Sheila Deare.

"You're back then, inspector."

"As you say, Miss Deare. And I see you've been assisting my colleague here to make a start."

"Well, you know my feelings on that, inspector," replied Sheila shortly. "So I will leave you to give her whatever orders you see fit." She brushed past Constable, and the library door closed behind her with a firm thud.

"Not in the happiest of moods, I think," commented the inspector. "I hope she hasn't been putting obstacles in your way, Singleton."

"Not at all, sir. Not that she's had much of a

chance. I've not long been here."

"Well, anyway, thank you for turning out on what I gather was your day off. It's good to see you again."

"You too, sir." Una's eyes met Dave Copper's. "Sergeant."

"Sergeant," he responded.

"Oh, for goodness sake, enough of the 'sergeant, sergeant' business," said Constable. "I haven't been a detective for goodness-knows-how-many-years without being able to spot when there's something going on in front of my eyes. So as long as the relationship remains entirely professional when it comes to work, I have no interest in delving further. Okay?"

"Okay, sir," dimpled Una.

"Yes, guv. Er ... thanks, guv."

"So, back to our muttons. What have we got, Singleton?"

"Well, like I say, sir," said Una, "I've not really got going. I was just about to check the murder weapon for prints, but I have to say, I'm not particularly hopeful, on account of that." She pointed to a white dinner-napkin lying half-concealed under the desk, which looked to have slight traces of red on it. "At a guess, that may have been used to hold the knife, or at least to wipe off the handle after it had been used. And I assume it's come from those sandwiches up there." A small plate of sandwiches lay untouched on the library desk. "But that's as far as I've got."

"Then I think the best thing we can do is

leave you to carry on," said Constable. He glanced uneasily at the body. "Perhaps when you've finished the personal examination, it might be a kindness to find something to cover the victim. I can't help feeling it's undignified to leave her just lying there. And after you've finished here, I think it would be a good idea if you were to turn your attention to Mrs. Ronson's room upstairs. I expect we can persuade Inspector Deare to show you the way."

"Leave it to me, sir." Una turned back to her task.

"Which reminds me, I need to speak to her about something else. I'll look forward to your report later. Come along, Copper. Let's let the lady concentrate." Constable, his junior in tow, returned to the hall, where Sheila Deare, her features still wearing a scowl of disapproval, had taken over Phil Knightly's chair behind the reception desk. The inspector took a seat in one of the armchairs on the other side of the desk.

"Look, Sheila," he began in an effort to mollify the security officer, "I know you don't agree with my bringing in extra personnel, but we are both on the same side in this. It's in your interests as well as mine to get this wrapped up as quickly as we can, and you know that SOCO would have to be involved sooner or later, so why not make it sooner so that, with a bit of luck, we can present a solution to the problem before it hits the news. Sensible?"

Sheila sighed. "I suppose so, Andy. So, did you make any progress in the village?"

"Perhaps rather more than I expected," responded Constable. "I have a couple of things I'd like to clear up. And the first of those is what happened when the Prime Minister's car first arrived in Dammett Worthy. She went into the church. Was this planned?"

"No, not at all. It's just that we were driving by, and she noticed one of the ministerial cars parked outside, and she said that she wondered who that was."

"She didn't recognise whose car it was?"

"No. They're all pretty much identical, but I know all the registration numbers, so I told her it was Perry Neal. And straight away she told the driver to stop, and then she got out and went into the church."

"You didn't accompany her?"

"No," said Sheila. "She said she had a little private communing to do. Slightly out of character, I thought – she'd never struck me as particularly religious - but as there wasn't another soul in sight, I judged that there wasn't any threat to her safety. So I stayed in the car. And then a little while after that, Dr. Neal came out and got into his car, and a short while after that, Mrs. Ronson herself emerged, and we continued on to the Hall."

"She didn't say anything about her visit to the church?"

"Not a word. Well, not to me. She settled back in her seat looking out of the window, and I thought I heard her murmur something about 'Hippocratic', or some such – I assumed she must have meant the Hippocratic oath, which I thought must have been some reference to Dr. Neal, but she didn't seem disposed to chat, so that was it until we arrived here a few minutes later."

"How about when everybody adjourned to the Dammett Well Inn in the evening for dinner? Was there anything said then that might have some bearing on what was happening between the ministers?" enquired Constable.

"I really couldn't tell you, I'm afraid, Andy," replied Sheila. "I wasn't in the dining room during the meal. I stayed outside in the bar and had something to eat there. It gave me the chance to make sure that nobody unauthorised strayed into the dining room. Only Mr. Porter and the two waiting staff were allowed in there."

"Just as a matter of interest, Sheila, did you carry out any checks into the Dammett Well staff before you arranged the dinner?"

"Only cursory ones into the landlord and his waitress." Sheila gave the ghost of a smile. "I couldn't imagine that the Dammett Worthy village pub would be the secret haunt of rabid revolutionaries, so it didn't seem necessary to do anything more rigorous."

"Hmmm." Andy Constable's lack of comment was eloquent.

"I know what you're thinking, Andy," said Sheila ruefully. "And you're quite right. I'm just worried about the ramifications of the whole business. And for me personally, too. Obviously the Prime Minister's security was not what it should have been."

Constable smiled wryly. "You speak truer than you know, Sheila. And not for the obvious reason."

Sheila frowned. "I don't know what you mean."

"Tell me, how far did your remit extend as far as Mrs. Ronson's security was involved?"

"Just her personally. Why?"

"So not extending to the staff around her? I mean in Whitehall."

"No. There's a unit that deals with that sort of thing." Sheila continued to look puzzled. "I don't see what you're getting at."

"The fact is, Sheila," said Constable, "you have a cuckoo in the nest." And as Sheila's bafflement grew, "Can you just jot something down for me? Anything will do. 'The quick brown fox' or something."

Sheila, plainly still not understanding, reached for a sheet of paper on the desk and scribbled a few words. "Will that do?"

Constable glanced at the handwriting. "As I thought. Someone had sent a note to try to warn the P.M. about the interloper, but that someone was evidently not you. Not, I suppose, that it matters particularly, because if someone was trying to protect Mrs. Ronson, they probably wouldn't be likely to want to kill her. However, someone at Number 10 is going to catch a very severe cold for employing an undercover journalist so close to the Prime Minister. Whether that affects this case, I'm about to go and find out."

Sheila had a look of complete astonishment written all over her face. "But who is it you're talking about? Not one of the ministers, surely?"

"No. It is in fact your waiter, Jim Daly."

"What?"

Constable nodded. "His actual name is Seamus Daly. He works for one of the tabloids. And, if he's still ensconced in the morning room, I'm off to have a little word with him." He stood. "Come along, Copper. Notebook at the ready. I think Mr. Daly is going to have to do a little extra reporting." He made for the door of the morning room, leaving Sheila Deare looking profoundly concerned.

*

"You've not been entirely honest with me, Mr. Daly, have you?" challenged Andy Constable, as he strode into the room, to find Jim Daly still with his feet up on the sofa.

"Ah." Jim swung his feet round to sit upright. "I wondered how long it would be before we had this little chat."

"Possibly not as long as you would have liked, Mr. Daly. So let's talk about your real job and what you're doing here." Constable seated himself and gave Jim a hard stare.

"Ah well, nothing is forever." Jim shrugged philosophically. "Except maybe diamonds. But certainly not the late Diamond Doris." He winced. "Apologies, inspector. That was a remark in very poor taste. Actually, for all that I had to do with her, I quite liked the woman. And it was a good gig while it lasted. But in answer to your question, inspector, I have been honest with you, in that I haven't told you a word of a lie. But I'll grant you, I may not have been entirely candid."

"So let's elicit a few facts, without embroidery, if you please, Mr. Daly," said Constable, indicating to Dave Copper to take notes. "And just for the avoidance of doubt, since you're a journalist, you should be aware that this conversation is very much on the record."

"Am I under caution?"

"No, you are not, Mr. Daly," retorted Constable, beginning to allow a touch of exasperation to show. "I have no reason to suppose that you are guilty of anything other than what some might see as a breathtaking level of deceit. So please, can I have some straight answers?"

Jim thought for a moment, and then gave an open and guileless smile. "Sorry, inspector. Force of habit, dancing around the truth. But as my cover is now completely blown, ask away."

"Right then, ..." began the inspector.

"Oh, just one thing," interrupted Jim. "Is there any chance that, when this is all sorted out, I can have an exclusive interview?"

"Don't push your luck," growled Constable. "And you can consider yourself fortunate if I don't put you on a charge for wasting police time." He drew a deep breath. "So, we'll start again. You're a reporter. You have a regular column in the 'Daily Globe'. So how and why did you come to be working at Number 10?"

"Oh, there's no mystery at all about that, inspector. As for the why, surely it's obvious. With everything that's been going on in politics lately, and all these people working together who'd been at daggers drawn previously, there had to be a very tasty inside story as to what was happening at the heart of the government. And what sort of journalist would I be if I didn't want to go after it?"

"Do you really want an answer to that question, Mr. Daly?"

Jim grinned. "Probably best not. But as for the how, I told you. I knew somebody who knew somebody, and it was the easiest thing in the world to wangle my way on to the government payroll as one of the menials. Don't you remember that story a few years ago about the guy who got a job at Buckingham Palace? One of my rivals from another rag. He wanted to see if there was anything going on behind the scenes in the royal household that he could spill the beans about, no doubt to the great delight of his slavering readers, so he managed to get himself taken on as a footman. Pretty low grade, but it still got him access to all sorts of little bits and pieces, including what the royals like for breakfast and who does what with the toothpaste. Not exactly earth-shattering stuff, but the public lapped it up. So I had the idea, if it worked for him, why not for me? In my book, no idea is too good to pinch. And there's a lot more power swilling around in the corridors of Whitehall, so I figured there was a lot more scope for skulduggery." Jim smiled contentedly. "Too right, there was. If I can't get a book deal out of this, I deserve to be back on the bottom rung of the ladder covering dog shows. But as it is, I think my editor is going to welcome me back with open arms."

"Your welcome at your newspaper doesn't interest me in the slightest, Mr. Daly," said Constable sharply. "What I wish to know is, what information can you give me about the people in this case?"

"But I've told you all I know about what happened over the dinner last night," protested Jim. "And I've not been around the house at all, until this morning."

"I'm not talking about the last twenty-four hours. I mean previously. If you're anything like worth your salt as a reporter, surely there will be things you have discovered that could point to who might have wanted Mrs. Ronson dead. In my experience, there are very few reasons for people to kill, other than the random violence of the moment. One main motive is gain. People commit murder either for simply financial reasons, or else to advance themselves by removing an obstacle. The other motive is protection. They kill either to protect someone else from a threat, or to counteract a danger to themselves. Physical or reputational."

"Ah," said Jim. "And in the murky world of politics, the reputation must be protected at all costs. Is that what you're saying, inspector?"

"It is."

"And that's where I come in? You reckon I've got the dirty on all our candidates for the handcuffs?"

"I'm hoping so, Mr. Daly. So, have you?"

Jim thought for a few seconds and then sighed. "You know, inspector, if you weren't a policeman, you'd make a pretty good reporter." Constable gazed at him stonily. "That's a compliment, by the way. Because you don't look as if you'll let go of something once you've got your teeth into it." A deep breath. "Okay, if I tell you what I know, I'm going to have to trust you not to spill the beans to all and sundry about everyone and spoil my story. After all, even a humble hack's got to make a living."

"No promises, Mr. Daly. But if you have information about someone that's not relevant to this specific case, I can't see why I should be stealing your thunder by revealing it to anyone else."

"If that's as good as it gets, I'll take it. Mind you, some of the things I have so far are just whispers, and I haven't got too much detail. But ask me your questions. Who do you need to know about?"

Constable turned to his junior colleague. "Copper, you've got a note of the ministers in the order we spoke to them. We might as well go down the list. Who was first?"

"That was Mrs. Nye, sir."

"Well, Mr. Daly?"

"The lady in charge of the justice system, eh? Well, as far as I know, she's as pure as the driven snow. You'd expect someone to have some skeletons lurking in a closet somewhere, but I haven't found any relating to her. Mind you, I wouldn't be quite so sure about that husband of hers. Not that I've had a chance to go ferreting about at all, but I've seen him at one of those Downing Street do's, and he struck me as a pretty slippery character. And there are murmurs. He's in finance somewhere in the City, I believe, and you know what everyone says about bankers."

Jim's remark struck a chord with something in the back of Constable's mind. "Thank you for that. Who's next, Copper?"

"Mr. Grade, sir. Who happened to be sat next to Mrs. Nye at dinner."

"Yes, I remember we've already been told a couple of things about him. So perhaps we can move on to the next one. Which is ...?"

"That's Amanda Laye, guv."

"Who has just come back from her overseas trip. The Far East, if I remember correctly. Although I seem to recall being told about a couple of mentions of the Middle East. Something to do with a knowledge of Arab cuisine."

"Well, that wouldn't surprise me the tiniest bit," scoffed Jim. "Not with that lady."

"And why would that be, Mr. Daly?" enquired Constable, scenting revelations.

"Sure, and it didn't take a lot of digging to find out that when she was a student at Camford University, she was extremely friendly with a certain Arab prince who was the eldest son of the

Emir of Kujaira. Nothing wrong in that, of course, and that's no doubt where she acquired an intimate knowledge of Middle Eastern cuisine, and a few other things besides, if my sources are to be trusted. You might say that there was no gulf between the two students, as it were."

"But isn't that just gossip? Why would a student romance from years ago be of any interest now?"

"No interest at all normally, inspector. Except that the lady is now Foreign Secretary, and the boy who was the prince is now the reigning Emir. And that is a very sensitive part of the world. You join the dots."

"Nothing's simple, is it?" Constable asked himself half-aloud. "So, moving on, sergeant, what's the next name?"

"Mrs. Hayste, sir."

"Our Marion? Something of a dark horse," remarked Jim. "Very much in the shadow of her boss, it seems to me. I know there's something going on about a new initiative on prisons – drugs, I think - but I haven't managed to crowbar anything useful out of anyone yet."

"Mr. Knightly did mention something about words passing between her and Mrs. Nye before the party left for the pub, sir," offered Copper. "Possibly slightly heated. If that's any help."

"That might account for the fact that she seemed somewhat subdued over dinner, inspector," suggested Jim. "Even when I was about to top up her glass of water, DiDo looked across and said something like 'Not more watering down, surely?', but Marion didn't answer. I don't know that I heard much out of her at all. So, sorry, I've no extra dirt to dish."

"Then we come to whoever is next." Constable turned to his junior. "Sergeant, this list seems to go on forever."

"Only a couple more, guv," Copper reassured him. "This one's Dr. Neal."

"Charming chap," commented Jim. "Probably because he's got no background in politics. I can't think of anything extra I know about him, inspector. Maybe I should have gone rooting into his history in his old local papers."

"Don't worry about that, Mr. Daly," replied Constable. "I think we've been told quite enough to think about for the time being. So that brings us to ...?"

"Erica Mayall, sir."

"Ah, the one with expensive tastes. I reckon you've had plenty from me on the subject of that lady," said Jim. "I told you what was said over dinner. I'm sure, with a little gentle research of your own, you can work out how things stood between her and Mrs. Ronson."

"Oh. Very well," said Constable, slightly disconcerted by the response. "Which I'm sincerely hoping brings us to the last of our ministers."

"It does, sir," confirmed Copper. "Mr. Fitt."

"Our East End boy," said Jim.

"Although I think he told us he was quite pleased to move on from there when we spoke to him," observed Constable.

"Ah, well, maybe he hasn't moved on quite far enough for his liking, inspector, if some of the whispers I hear turn out to be true. One of my sources promised me the mother of all revelations. That was on my to-do list we got back to Westminster."

"Weren't we told of a couple of remarks Mrs. Ronson made to Mr. Fitt, sir?" Copper reminded his superior. "There was something Gideon Porter heard, and also one of the others. I'm sure I've got it in my notes somewhere." He started to leaf back through his notebook.

Constable took a decision. "Save it for now, sergeant. We'll be going back over everything in due course anyway, but at the moment, I'm starting to suffer from information overload. I think a medicinal cup of tea and a biscuit is the least we can expect Mr. Knightly to provide for us out of the hotel's facilities." He rose. "Let's see if we can roust him out."

"Does that mean you're finished with me, inspector?" asked Jim. "Any chance I can be on my way?"

"Not a hope," retorted Constable. "My brain is not so fuddled that I'm prepared to let a journalist in possession of some sensational news loose on the world. I'm afraid you're going to have to cool your heels here a little longer. But I can arrange for a refill of your coffee pot, if that will help."

"You're too kind." Jim settled back again in his customary reclining position.

"Oh, just one thing." Constable paused in

the doorway. "Would you happen to know of someone called Heather? The name's cropped up out of nowhere on a piece of the hotel's stationery among Mrs. Ronson's belongings, and I can't see why it should. It's not as if we've got any Heathers in the mix."

Jim laughed. "Ah, inspector, it's plain you're no gardener."

"And you are?" The inspector raised a doubting eyebrow.

"What, you don't see me getting my hands dirty down in the mud?" said Jim. "Well, maybe not in the literal sense anyway. You probably think otherwise."

"So what on earth has gardening got to do with anything?" asked Constable, perplexed.

"My old mam could tell you in a minute," said Jim. "Very fond of her garden, she is. Especially her heather garden. Her pride and joy, that is. As kids, we all had to go and admire it on a regular basis."

"And so ...?"

"Oh, come on, Mr. Constable," teased Jim. "Call yourself a detective? You can't expect me to do all the hard work for you. But I bet if you take a look in the library, you'll probably find some sort of reference book on plants or botany. That'll sort your Heather out soon enough."

Chapter 11

Phil Knightly was just replacing the telephone receiver as the two detectives entered his office. He looked weary.

"Not interrupting at a bad time, Mr. Knightly, I hope," said Andy Constable.

"Not at all, Mr. Constable," replied Phil. "In fact, that was the last of the guests I've had to put off." He attempted a rather sketchy smile. "I'm beginning to think, with all the lies and evasions I've had to come up with, I should be contemplating a career in crime. I'm sure it would be less complicated than my life at present."

"Best stay as you are, sir," said Constable, echoing the smile. "Sergeant Copper and I have a pretty formidable clear-up rate, you know."

The hotel manager grimaced. "Thanks for the advice, inspector. How about the clear-up of our current problem? Are you getting anywhere on that?"

"We're making progress, sir," answered Constable. "That's the best I can tell you at present."

Phil turned to his computer. "Anyway, my guest problem is at least postponed, so that's one job done." He started to click keys. "Now, what can I do for you?"

"For a start, sir, don't close your computer down too irrevocably. We're going to want to use it to take a look at something."

"Oh? What, now?" Phil's hand hovered over the keyboard.

"Not just at this second, sir. As far as Sergeant Copper and I are concerned, the main priority at the moment is sustenance. I think we may be in danger of running out of fuel, and I wondered if we could prevail on you to organise a cup of tea for us. Maybe even a biscuit or two?"

"That, inspector, is the most refreshingly normal thing anyone's said to me today. Yes, of course, I'll be glad to. Do you want me to bring it through to the drawing room?"

"No, that's fine, sir. We'll come through to the kitchen with you, if that's all right."

"By all means." Phil stood and turned to open what looked like a cupboard door behind his desk. "Come on through."

"You know, guv, I'd forgotten that little door to the kitchen existed," remarked Dave Copper as the police officers made to follow the hotel manager. "What with hidden doors and secret staircases, this place is a bit of a rabbit warren, isn't it?"

"All designed to make our job more fun," agreed Constable.

As the three entered the kitchen, the inspector was slightly surprised to find Sheila Deare seated at the table gazing moodily into a mug of tea.

"We've obviously had identical thought processes, Sheila," commented Constable. "Nothing like tea to refresh a policeman's brain. Or woman's," he added swiftly.

"There's still some in the pot," responded Sheila. "Although it's probably rather stewed by now."

"Don't worry, I'll make fresh," said Phil, and busied himself with a clatter in the background.

"So where do we stand, Andy?" asked Sheila.

"Questions and answers, questions and answers," replied Constable. "Rather more of the former than the latter for now, but I've got a few thoughts beginning to coalesce in my mind. My next step is to go and have a further word with our happy band of virtual prisoners upstairs to see if I can refine any of those thoughts, but Copper and I were in need of a little re-fuelling, so we've enlisted Mr. Knightly's services." He looked over his shoulder. "Oh, by the way, sir, maybe it might be a good idea to provide the ministers with something to go on with in terms of lunch."

"I could organise some sandwiches," suggested Phil.

"Excellent idea, sir," approved Constable. "I don't want people fainting from malnutrition. And could you possibly add some coffee to the order and see it gets to Mr. Daly in the morning room? I think he probably deserves some reward for what he's been able to tell us."

"What, despite the fact that he's here under false pretences?" Sheila sounded outraged. "He should think himself lucky that he's not under arrest, but he's obviously out of it, since I'm his alibi. But in my opinion, all he deserves is a kick up the ..."

"Take the positive view, Sheila," interrupted Constable quickly, as Phil placed cups of tea and a plate of biscuits in front of the detectives. "He's been able to give us information that wouldn't have come our way if he weren't who he is. So I'm grateful for that. Anyway, how about yourself? What's the latest with you?"

"Not that much," confided Sheila. "I looked in to the library just now, but your Sergeant Singleton was still busy in there. She said she hoped not to be too much longer and she'd let me know when she was ready to move on to Mrs. Ronson's room, so as my presence seemed surplus to requirements, I thought I'd come and have a cup of tea in here and contemplate my future. Besides, I didn't want to hang around in a room where someone had been murdered."

Dave Copper exchanged glances with his superior and cleared his throat. "Oh, if only you knew," he muttered through crumbs.

Constable gulped the last of his tea. "That reminds me. Copper, get on to the doc, would you? Check where the van he said he'd send to remove the remains has got to. I'd like to give him the chance to confirm his findings as soon as possible, before he actually retires. Then you can come and find me. I'll be in the library." He stood and opened what he thought was the door through which the detectives had entered, to find himself looking at the lower treads of a narrow winding staircase. "Mr. Knightly, help me out. I'm getting confused with all these doors. Which is my best route?"

"Not that one, inspector," said Phil, "Unless you're heading up to the bedrooms. Just go through that door over there that actually looks like a door, and you'll find yourself in the dining room corridor. Turn left, and you'll be out in the hall."

Copper turned back from the corner, where he had been murmuring into his mobile. "Quick and easy, sir. According to the doc, the meat-wagon ..." He broke off at Constable's growl of disapproval. "Sorry, sir. What I meant to say was, the pathologist's van has just come through the gates. It's on its way up the drive even as we speak."

"Good. Sheila, could you perhaps go out to meet them and bring them through to the library?"

"Of course, Andy. And then I suppose I'd better check in with my masters in Whitehall. They'll be hopping up and down wanting anything I can tell them."

"Fob them off for a little while longer as best you can," suggested Constable. "Copper and I will do our damnedest to drive this forward as fast as possible. I can't help thinking I'm starting to get a few gleams of light at the end of the tunnel, but they're rather dimmer than I would wish. Come along, sergeant – notebook at the ready, and we'll go and jemmy a few more pieces of information out of our cast of suspects. That's after we've checked in with your ... with Sergeant Singleton."

In the library, Una Singleton was seated behind the desk, tapping entries into her tablet computer. She looked up as the detectives entered.

"How's it going, sergeant?" Constable was uncomfortably aware of the now sheet-draped body of the late Prime Minister still sprawled on the floor, a mute reproach to those charged with uncovering her murderer.

"Pretty well, sir," she replied. "I was just typing up the last of my notes."

"Which is excellent timing, because the doctor's van is just arriving to remove the body."

"Do you want a report on what I've got so far, sir?"

"Not at the moment. We all have other fish to fry. I want you to take a look at the Prime Minister's room while I'm having another talk with her colleagues. So follow us." Constable led the way out of the room and up the stairs, just as Sheila Deare was ushering two of the doctor's sombrely-dressed staff in through the front door. At the head of the stairs, Constable pointed to the left. "The room you want is at the end of the corridor," he said. "The Chinese Bedroom. Do you want Sergeant Copper to help you find it?"

"That's fine, sir," smiled Una. "I'm sure I can find my way into a bedroom without needing David's help."

"Then we will leave you to get on," said Constable, ignoring the choking noises coming from his junior colleague behind him. "And we will make a start at the far end, and rendezvous with you when we're finished. Come along ... David ... refresh my memory. Who's our first port of call?"

Copper leafed back through his notes. "That's Mr. Fitt, sir."

"Off we go, then."

*

When he answered the door of the Cedar Room, Benny seemed to have lost some of his robust jocularity. His still shiny features looked careworn.

"Is anything happening?" he enquired of the detectives as they entered the room.

"Enquiries are progressing, Mr. Fitt," said Andy Constable, taking a stance in front of the fireplace, Dave Copper at his side. "But there are one or two things that I'd like to clarify if I may. Just as I'm doing with all your other colleagues. And as I know that you are keen on not keeping people waiting too long, I thought we'd come to you first."

"That's kind of you, inspector." Benny's smile was slightly off-key. "So what would you like to know?"

"You left us with the impression that relations between the Prime Minister and all your other colleagues were largely amicable, Mr. Fitt."

"Well, other than the normal fencing over the odd territorial dispute between departments, that's true," said Benny warily. "Why, has someone been saying something different?"

"Quite a few people, sir. And one person in

particular heard some words pass between Mrs. Ronson and yourself which shed a slightly different light on the matter. Something to do with a lady living in the constituency of your P.P.S. Who might that be, I wonder? And why would it matter to you?"

"Oh, please, inspector. I can't be expected to keep all the individual cases involving my department in my head."

"Of course not, sir. Nobody would expect you to. But this was also in the wake of some other remarks which had been made concerning families in your journey down to the pub. So I'm getting the impression that Mrs. Ronson may not have been entirely satisfied that your department's family policy was going in the right direction. Perhaps she was demanding a change. And perhaps she felt that someone other than yourself would be a better person to enact this change. In other words, isn't it possible that your job was on the line? Could I be justified in thinking that you were about to be dismissed? And couldn't that give you a very sound motive, in your own mind, for killing the woman who held your fate in her hands?"

"This is all nonsense!" blustered Benny. "Why on earth would I want to murder the P.M. over some woman in Whitechapel, whoever she may be?"

*

"He's badly rattled, guv," remarked Copper, as the two officers stood once again in the corridor.

"That he most certainly is," agreed Constable, "and yet he has a point. Why should one specific case be the basis of a threat to his career? There's a piece of the jigsaw missing. And I'm wondering if it's anything to do with these whispers that Mr. Daly was talking about. More thought required, I think, but in the meantime, let's move on."

Erica Mayall had changed from the exotic informal dressing gown she had been wearing earlier into a dramatic but sombre midnight-blue dress with a severely cinched-in waist, to which had been added a touch of glamour by means of a shot-silk pashmina in shades of purple casually draped around her shoulders. Her purple and gold footwear sported vertiginously high heels. Heavy gold jewellery with a hint of the barbaric adorned her wrist and ears. In response to the detectives' request to enter, she stood back wordlessly, seated herself in her previous position on the sofa, crossed her legs, and gazed up at Constable in expectant silence.

"If I may say so, Ms. Mayall, you are managing to maintain your composure very well in the face of this tragedy," began Constable. "Some people would be quite ruffled by the situation, and yet here you are, still succeeding in looking remarkably chic. Something of an achievement. Particularly in view of your close relationship with Mrs. Ronson."

Erica's flawlessly made-up features did not move. "We had a great deal in common, inspector."

"But you also had disagreements, I think. And for some reason, I keep hearing the word 'shoes' crop up." Constable glanced down at Erica's feet. "I must say, if those you're wearing are typical of your style, I can understand why they would draw attention. Now, without wishing to be disrespectful of the dead, I think we can agree that nobody would have described the late Prime Minister as a fashion leader. She probably did not regard her personal appearance as being of prime importance in the carrying out of her rôle. You, on the other hand, are in a much more prominent situation with reference to the position of women in public life. One might almost say you are – and please don't bite my head off for using the expression – something of a poster-girl." Erica's glare was a clear indication of her opinion of Constable's choice of words. "But," the inspector pressed on, "maintaining a first-class visual image doesn't necessarily come cheap. And you've been described to me as a lady with tastes which come at considerable expense. I'm just wondering if the word expense was used coincidentally in that context."

"I have no idea what you're driving at, inspector," responded Erica.

"Oh, I think you do, Ms. Mayall," countered Constable. "Overseas trips are costly. We're all aware of how toxic the matter of M.P.'s expenses can be. People's careers have been destroyed. Is it possible that Mrs. Ronson felt that yours could become one of those casualties? Might she have decided to nip a problem in the bud before it became public? And might you not have decided to make a pre-emptive strike?"

"You have no idea how ridiculous this sounds, Mr. Constable," asserted Erica, ice in her tone.

"Perhaps it does, Miss Mayall," conceded the inspector. "As I've said, you two were close." Suddenly recalling one of Jim's earlier observations, he elected to try a wild shot in the dark. "Perhaps very close. More than close, even?"

There was an extremely long pause.

Erica's face suddenly crumpled, before she took a deep breath and steadied herself. "You can put away any prejudices, inspector," she replied in a slightly shaky voice. "They won't be needed here." She hesitated as if seeking the right words, and her tone strengthened. "There was nothing physical about our friendship. Nothing that was ever even put into words. I don't think either of us even thought of such a thing. But one evening, after a particularly long day in the House of Commons over one of the former government's measures, we went back to her office to talk over the situation. And that's all. We talked. But in one of the pauses in the conversation, there came one of those moments. We just looked at one another. I didn't say anything. Neither did she. And I'm not sure what we would have said anyway. But we both knew. It wasn't an emotion I'd ever felt before, and I sensed that neither had she. She'd been a happily-married woman, for goodness' sake. But after that, we've always ... cared for one another. I don't know how else to put it. But I'm confident that it never affected our professional relationship. Or my career. I just know that it means that she would never have done anything to injure me, and I would certainly never have harmed her."

"I don't know how well that accords with one of Mrs. Ronson's remarks that anything that you'd been given could easily be taken away," observed Constable. "A rather sharp put-down, by the sound of it. So hardly a rose without a thorn."

"Think what you like, inspector. I know what I know."

"Of course, there is also one fact which doesn't seem to fit into this situation. Or rather, one person. So perhaps you can enlighten me. Who is Heather?"

Erica's face set. She clamped her lips shut and made no answer.

"You see," continued the inspector, "the picture you paint is very compelling. A caring platonic relationship where nothing inappropriate intrudes. But let me indulge in a little wild speculation. What if another person were to intrude? What if this undeclared affection were jeopardised by the appearance of a third person? Someone who perhaps dripped the poison concerning your personal extravagance, for example? Someone who threatened to tear down the structure that had been so carefully created? And supplant it with herself? There is a saying about hell having no fury, and so on. So might a woman who faced the situation I describe, take it into her head to strike first? 'If I cannot have what I want, then nobody shall'? Can't you see, Ms. Mayall, that, in the hands of a determined prosecutor, this could all look only too plausible?"

"You have no idea what you're talking about, Mr. Constable," said Erica, still stony-faced. "And before you make yourself even more ridiculous by conjuring up any more wild fantasies, I suggest you go." She marched to the door and held it open, glaring defiantly as the two police officers left the room.

*

There was silence for a few moments.

"I'm not sure that went exactly according to plan, did it, guv?" ventured Dave Copper eventually.

Andy Constable sighed in exasperation. "Very little of it did, to be perfectly honest. But we've elicited a few more facts that explain some of the things that people have overheard in dribs and drabs."

Copper had a thought. "Tell you one thing, sir. It all accounts very nicely for that letter I found in Mrs. Ronson's room – you know, the reply to a resignation. Obviously that would refer to Ms. Mayall."

"Would it, though?" Constable sounded dubious. "I'm not convinced. The potential for personal scandal, well, maybe. You know how prim the public can be. But that would only be if the story were publicised and provable, and I'm not sure either of those applies."

"What about the jealousy aspect, guv? How much of that last bit you put forward do you think is actually true?"

"To be frank, sergeant, very little," admitted Constable. "It was something of a flight of fancy. A bow at a venture, if you like. But it doesn't answer my question as to the identity of this 'Heather'."

"Well, she's got to be one of the other women in the house, hasn't she, sir?" said Copper reasonably. "If that note was on the hotel's headed paper, it couldn't have pre-dated their arrival here."

"Good point. Well, at least that narrows it down. Maybe we'll shed some light on the matter when we get the chance to take up Mr. Daly's suggestion of checking in the library. But in the meantime, we'd better carry on. His Lordship's Room is next, I see. That's Dr. Neal, isn't it?"

Perry Neal took a few moments to answer his door. "Oh, Mr. Constable. Come in, come in. You too, sergeant." He ushered the detectives into the room. "You'll have to forgive me, inspector," he said, rubbing his eyes. "But do you know, I must have dozed off. One of the hazards of approaching age, you know. I'd put some music on the radio to relax, and the next thing I know, you're tapping at my door. And I have no idea what time it is." He looked at his watch. "Gracious!"

"Yes, sir, the time is getting on," agreed Constable. "And it must be very tedious for you, being kept confined here in your room, but I'm afraid I don't really have any other option but to insist upon it."

"But the question is," asked the minister, "is it proving productive? Are you getting anywhere?"

"I hope we're beginning to, sir."

"Well, sit down and tell me." Perry indicated the sofa, and the officers resumed their earlier places.

"Actually, it's rather more a case of asking than telling, Dr. Neal," said Constable. "We've received quite a lot of extra information, and what I'm seeking now are the facts which join everything up into a coherent whole."

"Such as?"

"Such as, sir, the fact that you didn't mention to us that you'd had an encounter with the Prime Minister yesterday afternoon before you even arrived here at the Hall."

Perry looked slightly disconcerted. "That's true, inspector. How on earth did you know?"

"You were recognised, sir. The vicar had seen you on television recently."

"Oh. Is that all? Well, yes, I popped into the church on my way here, but I didn't tell you because I didn't think it was relevant. I didn't want to overburden you with matters that had no bearing on your investigations."

"I think I prefer to be the judge of what has a bearing and what doesn't, sir," replied Constable bluntly. "Particularly when I'm investigating a death, and death was the topic of the conversation which you had with Mrs. Ronson yesterday."

"But how ... I don't see ..." Perry's puzzlement was plain.

"You were overheard, Dr. Neal. Inadvertently, but that doesn't alter the fact. And the exchange of words in the church between you and Mrs. Ronson does give me cause to wonder. She spoke of you praying for the forgiveness of sins, I think."

"Isn't that what everyone does in church, inspector?" Perry attempted a light laugh in which Constable thought he could detect considerable unease.

"It depends on how personal those sins are, sir. How close to home they touch. And I have the impression that what Mrs. Ronson said - on the subject of the death of a mother and child – was rather pointed. Why would that be, sir, do you think?"

"I ... I really can't imagine, Mr. Constable." The minister shifted awkwardly.

"Try a little harder, sir." Constable's voice was implacable.

Perry did not speak for several moments. "I can only think of one case, inspector. There was a child brought to me with some very ordinary symptoms. Nothing unusual at all, so she was sent home to recover. But as it turned out, there was more to the matter than met the eye, and the child died. It was very sad. Nobody was to blame. But the mother was so affected that she died shortly afterwards. And as they were both my patients, I suppose I have to take some responsibility." A heavy silence fell.

"A tragic case, sir," said Constable in sympathetic tones. "Would it have been widely known?"

"Why should it, inspector?"

"So why, I wonder, should Mrs. Ronson bring it up now? I don't suppose it would have been anything to do with the television programme the vicar said she had seen? Which centred on death."

"I tell you, I don't know, inspector," insisted Perry. He was beginning to sound increasingly agitated. "And I can't understand why you're badgering me about something that was dead and buried years ago. Haven't you got something better to do? Shouldn't you be more concerned with trying to find out who killed Doris Ronson?"

"Everything I'm doing is concentrated towards that end, Dr. Neal," replied Constable calmly. "And will continue to be." He rose and, Copper behind him, moved towards the door.

Chapter 12

"Wouldn't it be refreshing, sergeant," said Andy Constable, "to get a few straight answers out of some people instead of these perpetual evasions?"

"Well, they are politicians, guv," Dave Copper reminded him. "Isn't not giving straight answers what they do for a living?"

"Maybe so," retorted Constable grimly. "But we'll have the truth before the day's out, I swear. Right. Next we have ...?"

Copper consulted his notebook. "Mrs. Marion Hayste, sir. In the Red Room."

"Crack on, then, shall we?" Constable tapped at the door.

"Oh, you again, inspector," was Marion's slightly breathless reaction as she opened the door in response to the detective's knock. "Have you found out anything?"

"We've made some progress." Constable remained non-committal. "But I'm still piecing together all the facts of the matter. I wonder if we may come in?"

Marion glanced over her shoulder. "Yes, of course." She stood back.

"As far as we can tell," began the inspector, "you may have been the last person to see Mrs. Ronson alive. You were the last minister in for interview during that long session last night. So just on the off-chance that she may have let something slip regarding your colleagues, I think it might help me to know what you spoke about."

"I honestly can't talk about confidential government matters, inspector."

"I fear, Mrs. Hayste, that sometimes matters are not quite as confidential as we would wish. Let me take a guess – was it all about drugs, by any chance?"

Marion's eyes widened. "But ... how did you know?"

Constable smiled. "Official secrets aren't always completely secret, Mrs. Hayste. And I'm afraid that you have had in your midst an investigative journalist who seems to have ferreted out some information about your new drugs initiative for prisons."

Marion turned away and looked out of the window for several long seconds. She seemed to be mastering some emotion. Then she turned back to the inspector. "Lewis Stalker again, I suppose?" She sounded angry. "Are you going to tell me he's been going about, shooting his mouth off as usual about things which are nothing to do with him? You'd think he'd never heard of the Official Secrets Act."

Constable was surprised at the vehemence of Marion's reaction. "Don't be too quick to blame Mr. Stalker, madam," he replied. "He's not the one who told us. And in fact, we did hear from another source about words which passed between yourself and the Justice Secretary. It sounds as if they were on the same subject. As your departmental head, she would certainly have been entirely conversant with your activities, surely?"

"Dee?" Marion sounded reflective. "Yes, yes, of course she would. She knew all about it."

"We'll be having a chat with her a little later," said Constable, "so she'll confirm all this, no doubt." He smiled. "I say a little later. I hope I'm not being over-optimistic. We have several of your colleagues to speak to before we get to her. She's right at the far end of the corridor."

"Oh yes. The Blue Room. Very grand."

"So I come back to my initial question, Mrs. Hayste. When you spoke to Mrs. Ronson in the library last thing last night, did anything emerge during that conversation which might help me identify her killer?"

"But I don't see in what way?"

"Simply that they and Mrs. Ronson presumably would have a longer history than yourself. You said that you are a fairly new and junior member of the government. So I hoped that, as she possibly knew all your other colleagues better than you, she might have given an indication of any disharmony among them. It's a long shot, I know, but I hoped you might have been told something."

Marion turned her large dark eyes to the inspector. "Nothing, Mr. Constable. Nothing at all."

*

"Brick wall, guv." Dave Copper closed his notebook with a snap. "I haven't written down a thing. There wasn't anything worth writing."

"I'm not sure that's exactly true, sergeant,"

contradicted Andy Constable. "We have a couple of extra snippets. For a start, there's confirmation that this mysterious new policy was something to do with drugs in prisons. Goodness knows what relevance that may have, and it could well have nothing to do with the row which Phil Knightly overheard between Mrs. Hayste and her boss earlier in the evening, but it's a fact, so maybe it fits somewhere. Secondly, her very reticence flags up a thought in my mind. We've been told by a couple of people that she doesn't appear to have had a lot to say for herself during the course of the dinner last night. Now it could be that it's just what it appears on the surface – she mentioned that she's pretty much the most junior of the gathering, so she may simply have been intimidated by the more high-powered people around her. Maybe she's not the garrulous type. However, she was pretty quick to draw our attention to the fact that Lewis Stalker is. 'Shooting his mouth off', didn't she say?"

"She did, sir."

"Then since I believe the ebullient Mr. Stalker is to be found in the next room along, let's find out if he's got anything else he can shoot his mouth off to us about."

The door to the Indian Bedroom was flung wide, and Lewis Stalker greeted his visitors with a beaming smile. "Thank the lord! Somebody to talk to! Come in, inspector. You too sergeant." He bounced over to the television, switched it off, and threw himself into an armchair. "I've been reduced to watching daytime soaps to stave off the boredom. I could pretend that I'm doing research for my Culture and Media portfolio," he said with a chuckle, "but to be honest, it's all just chewing gum for the mind. Don't quote me, but I can't stand the majority of the rubbish they put on television most of the time, although the government is very grateful for the revenue it brings in, so I have to try to be slightly reticent. Doesn't always work, though, but please don't give me away. I'm going to have to rely on your discretion." He grinned frankly, while the detectives exchanged surreptitious looks. "However ... sit ye down, both. You'd better bring me up to date with what's happening, gentlemen, since I shall no doubt be doing the rounds of the studios when this is all over. So, tell all. All the news that's fit to print, anyway. Isn't that what they used to say?" He looked expectantly at Constable.

The inspector drew breath, grateful for the pause in Lew's flow of chatter. "I'm afraid, Mr. Stalker, that I'm likely to be a disappointment to you. It's going to be more a matter of asking questions on my part, rather than providing answers."

"Oh." Lew's face fell. "What a shame. Well, ask away, inspector. What is it you need to know? Although I think I've told you pretty much everything I can about yesterday."

"Maybe not quite everything, sir."

Lew furrowed his brow. "I can't think of anything I missed out."

"Can't you, sir? Well, let's see if I can

remind you. I think you told us that, as far as you were concerned, you and the Prime Minister had a perfectly normal conversation over dinner last night."

"Well, yes, I think so." The minister sounded more hesitant. "I couldn't repeat it word for word. And you don't always recollect exactly what you've said when you've had a glass or two of wine. Not that I was drunk, of course," he added hastily. "I hope nobody's been saying that I was."

"Not at all, sir," said Constable. "But what they have said is that there was something of a sharp exchange between Mrs. Ronson and yourself at one point in the meal. Do you remember that?"

"I really don't recall ..."

"Then I'll help you out, sir," pressed on Constable relentlessly. "Mrs. Ronson characterised something you had said as 'indefensible', we're told. I think there was mention of guards."

"Oh lord, yes. I remember. And Dee Nye came out with that hoary old '*Quis custodiet*' quote. Oh no, hold on – that was when she was putting Milo down over something he'd said. Ever ready to show off her erudition, is Dee, always eager to express an opinion on what everyone else is doing wrong, and she doesn't much care who's on the end of her sharp tongue."

"So you wouldn't want to be in her bad books over anything you'd said, sir?"

"Not likely! If she'd been a judge in the old days, she'd have had the black cap on before you could say 'knife'."

"So maybe Mrs. Nye will have caught something helpful, guv," intervened Copper. "She was seated nearby – she might have been paying attention."

"It's possible, sergeant. We'll have a word with her in due course, see what she has to say. However, we seem to be straying from the point a little, Mr. Stalker. It was what passed between Mrs. Ronson and yourself that I wanted to check on. So, what was it that you'd said that she believed was indefensible? I seem to remember the word cropping up more than once."

"The trouble is, inspector," said Lew, leaning forward confidentially, "I do so many interviews, it's sometimes a job to remember what I've been talking about and when. It could have been anything."

"Mrs. Ronson seems to have remembered it only too well, sir, if what we're told of her attitude towards it is anything to go by. But, unfortunately, she'll never be able to tell us what it was."

"She won't, will she, inspector?" There was a look in Lew's eyes which Constable could not define. "That must be very frustrating."

"Don't worry, sir. We've plenty of other areas we can explore."

"Speaking of which, is there any chance you might be letting us out of our rooms any time soon? I'm starting to feel a little stir-crazy, imprisoned in here."

Constable looked around the room. "Rather more a maharajah's palace than the Black Hole of Calcutta though, wouldn't you say, Mr. Stalker?" he remarked. "But no, I'm afraid that at this stage, I'd rather everyone stayed put."

"Well, someone seems to have had other ideas, inspector."

Constable frowned. "What do you mean by that, sir?"

"I'm sure I heard a door open and close a while back."

"When, sir?" asked the inspector sharply.

Lew shrugged. "Couldn't say exactly. The passage of time's all been a bit fluid since you cooped us all up. No proper landmarks, you see. Sometime before my lunch arrived."

"Any idea whose room it might have been? Close to, or further away?"

"I honestly couldn't tell you, inspector. It might have been anyone, and this corridor's a bit echoey. I really didn't pay that much attention. I just remember it registering in the back of my mind."

Constable sighed with impatience. "I distinctly remember asking everyone to stay in their rooms for the time being."

"Could have been Mr. Knightly, guv," pointed out Copper. "Either going into someone's room, or else in and out of those little secret stairs of his. He'll have been up and down with trays, won't he?"

"I hope you're right, sergeant. The last thing

I need is people wandering about unsupervised, treading all over our crime scene."

*

"Funny, isn't it, guv?"

"I can't say that I'm feeling particularly amused, sergeant," said Andy Constable.

"No, sir. What I mean is," explained Dave Copper, "the exceptionally chatty Mr. Stalker suddenly seems to have very little to say on the subject of his row, if that's what it was, with Mrs. Ronson. Now, to me, that looks very much as if there's something he doesn't want us to know."

"Which would be his motive for killing the Prime Minister, I assume?"

"You can't rule it out, can you, guv?" retorted Copper reasonably. "And after all, it's got to be one of them. Isn't he as good a candidate as any?"

"You're right, of course. And the number of jolly and cheerful hail-fellow-well-met murderers we've come across in our time certainly supports that. They aren't all swivel-eyed silent weirdos. Sadly for us, because it would make our job a great deal easier. However, ..." Constable squared his shoulders. "Life is as it is, and not as we would wish it to be. So, with that in mind, we'd better press on with our next call." He looked at the sign on the bedroom door. "Her Ladyship's Room. Wherein lurks ...?"

"The slightly terrifying Amanda Laye, sir."

"So she does. Not a particular happy lady, I seem to recall, when we first spoke to her. And I doubt if the passage of time has done much to remedy that situation. Let's just hope that Mr. Knightly will have managed to rustle up something for lunch which will have softened her mood. Well, deep breath, and in we go."

"Inspector Constable, this is becoming intolerable!" Amanda Laye's temper had clearly not improved in the way the detectives might have wished.

"I'm truly sorry ..." began the inspector.

"You simply cannot continue to hold me incommunicado in this way," swept on Amanda as if Constable had not spoken. "Or indeed any of us. But I in particular have matters that I have to attend to. As I may have mentioned, I have just returned from an extremely important overseas trip. My opposite numbers will have expected me to report my discussions with them and come back with a reaction from our government. This silence on my part will be inexplicable. There may be repercussions."

"Legal ones, madam?"

Amanda's heated flow stopped dead in its tracks. "What on earth do you mean, inspector?"

"I'm recalling a remark which Mrs. Ronson was heard to make to you, Miss Laye. It referred to your time as a student, and the gist of it was that it was unfortunate that you had not studied law at that time. I wonder why she might have said that?"

"I really can't remember ..." Amanda seemed to have become unexpectedly vague.

"Perhaps I could refresh your memory. It was over dinner. There was a Middle-Eastern style dish being served." Constable gave a bland smile. "Oh. There we go again. The subject of the Middle East cropping up once more. And not for the first time. Strange, since you told us that it formed no part of your most recent travels. Although I gather that you have contacts in that particular region."

"I have contacts throughout the world, inspector." Amanda had recovered her composure. "That would appear to be the nature of my job, wouldn't you say?"

"I'm sure it is, madam." Constable disregarded the hint of acid in the minister's tone. "And no doubt some of these contacts would be closer than others. Friends, one would hope. Particularly warm friends, in some instances?"

"Would you care to explain exactly what you are getting at, inspector?" said Amanda haughtily.

"Not what I am getting at, Miss Laye," replied Constable. "What interests me is what Mrs. Ronson was getting at when she made certain remarks to you. This mention of law intrigues me. Might she have been concerned over some of the legal aspects of our foreign policy? But," he continued before Amanda had a chance to interrupt, "these things are a long way above my pay grade. And fortunately, she will have had Mrs. Nye to consult on legal matters. Do you know, I may decide to ask if she has any thoughts in that area." He moved towards the door, leaving Amanda uncertain as to how to respond. He paused. "And I shall try not to keep you under restriction longer than I have to. Bearing in mind that I am working under direct orders from the Deputy P.M. in Downing Street. And as for any delay in pursuing your overseas liaisons, I'm sure your staff will be perfectly capable of staving off awkward questions. Isn't that what the Foreign Office does best?"

*

"Did you see those eyes, guv?" commented Dave Copper in an undertone, as the two detectives stood once again in the corridor. "When we first walked in. Definitely not a happy lady. I thought she was going to blast you on the spot."

"There was indeed a rather intimidating mixture of fire and ice," agreed Andy Constable with a rueful chuckle.

"Maybe those specs of hers have got safety glass in them," grinned Copper. "And that's what protected us from the Gorgon stare. Mind you, you did manage to take the wind out of her sails soon enough."

"A delightfully mixed metaphor, sergeant," smiled Constable. "One of your best so far, I think. But you're right. The level of outrage subsided surprisingly quickly."

"Why do you reckon that was, guv?"

"Well, I think it has nothing to do with geography and this recent trip of hers, no matter what she may say to draw our attention in that direction, and all to do with history, both long and medium-term."

"What, as in university term, sir?"

Constable laughed. "My compliments, Copper. Good pick-up. And you may well be right. I think we may have enough pieces to put together quite an interesting picture. One which could give us a reason why Miss Laye could find herself on the wrong side of the Prime Minister, with all that that implies. I will muse on the subject, once we've got our last couple of interviews out of the way. So, it's Mr. Grade next, isn't it?"

"It is, sir," confirmed Copper. "Our hotel manager's old pal."

"Or possibly not," demurred Constable. "Let's see what he has to say."

Milo Grade, propped up once again on his bed, was taking a bite from what appeared to be an enormous ham and tomato sandwich as the detectives entered his room in response to a rather muffled 'Come in!'. "Oh lord," he exclaimed untidily through the substantial mouthful. "Busted again. Every time you come in here, inspector, you find me lounging around eating. Well, it does something to pass the time, and this is a remarkably good sandwich." He polished off the remainder.

"I'm glad Mr. Knightly is looking after you so well, sir," said Constable affably. "I suppose it's only natural to take care of our old friends."

Milo pushed himself slightly more upright. "You said something before about me knowing him, didn't you, inspector?" he said with a faint hint of irritation in his tone. "And I think I told you then, I really don't remember him."

"I don't suppose it's important, sir," replied Constable. "I imagine it's the same at any large educational establishment – I mean, you would know that better than anyone, wouldn't you? Not that much mixing between courses, the Foodies not having much contact with the Spannermen, and so on. Or so I gather. Would that be one of the things you would want to address in your Department, I wonder?"

"I've got too many things on my plate to worry about social mixing at universities," said Milo irritably. "And I don't see how relevant it is to what you're supposed to be doing anyway, inspector. Surely you're here to talk about more important things than the work of my ministry."

"Ah, well that is where you would be wrong, sir," responded Constable, resuming his former position in one of the room's tub chairs and nodding to Copper to seat himself likewise. "Because the topic of your ministry's work cropped up during several conversations we've been told about."

"Really? I don't see ..."

"I think you and Mrs. Ronson exchanged words several times since your arrival here, didn't you, sir?" pressed on Constable.

"We spoke, certainly. That's what tends to happen when the Prime Minister summons her colleagues for a series of meetings, inspector," was Milo's acerbic retort.

"And if the snippets we've heard are accurate," continued Constable, unruffled by

Milo's attitude, "Mrs. Ronson seems to have been particularly concerned about the matter of fraud."

Milo looked disconcerted. "Well ... I mean ..." He bit his lip. "Oh, all right, inspector." He heaved a deep sigh. "I might as well be honest. Yes, it's a worry. There's been talk that annual national exam results haven't been all that they should be. And that some of the figures might have been massaged to make them look better than they actually are. But this is nothing to do with me. We're talking about the time before I took over the Department, so it can't be laid at my door. But that must be what people heard us talking about. And you can't seriously think that I would want to murder the P.M. over the failings of my predecessors. The idea's ludicrous. It just goes to prove that eavesdropping is a very unreliable source of information."

"That, sir, is unfortunately often very true, sir," agreed Constable. "But it doesn't take us away from the point that it sounds as if Mrs. Ronson was concerned about the matter. And I've been looking for any straws in the wind which indicate areas of conflict between the Prime Minister and her colleagues. However absurd. So let me speculate. There is a situation in schools which Mrs. Ronson finds intolerable. You are the minister in charge. You have a responsibility to put the matter right. But what if the P.M., for whatever reason, thinks you aren't up to the job? What if she decided, in the light of this meeting, that you should be getting your marching orders? That could well be a fatal blow to your career. And you're still relatively young for a minister – your career might never recover from such a setback, and then where would you be? So isn't it plausible that you might take drastic action to avoid that eventuality? Mightn't a man desperate to save his career decide to kill the woman who held his fate in her hands?"

"Over a bunch of school statistics?" scoffed Milo. "Oh really, inspector, this is beyond a farce! If your detecting skills can't come up with something better than that, then I think you should seriously consider a change of career."

*

"Our Mr. Grade seems to have lost his sense of humour, guv," remarked Dave Copper, not taking particular care to lower his voice as he pulled the door closed behind him. "And didn't he tell us that he gets flippant when he's nervous? Not much sign of that now, is there?"

"There is not," smiled Andy Constable in agreement. "But perhaps he snaps when he's really nervous."

"Of course, in one way, he hasn't got anything to be nervous about any more, has he?" mused Copper. "I mean, if he was worried that Mrs. Ronson was going to sack him, she certainly won't be doing that now. And he was pretty up-front – eventually – about this exams thing."

"Hmmm." Constable still sounded dubious. "In which case, what's troubling him? If he's prepared for us to consider the school results business, in which he says he is in the clear because it's all the fault of his predecessors, is he using that to distract our attention from something else? Maybe I should be taking his advice and putting my detecting skills to finding a better answer."

"That's one for your sitting-down-and-thinking session, isn't it, sir? I bet you've got one planned."

"Eventually, I hope. We shall go and find Sergeant Singleton to see what she has discovered, and with luck we shall be in a position to review all the information you've gathered together in that notebook of yours. Once we have disposed of this seemingly endless parade of interviewees, of course."

"I can't offhand remember a case where we've had quite so many people in line to talk to, guv," remarked Copper. "Thank goodness there's just the one to go."

"Ah, yes. Mrs. Nye. There were a couple of things I wanted to cross-check with her, weren't there?" Constable gave a brisk rap at the door of the Blue Room. There was no answer. "Oh, for goodness sake, don't say she's gone off somewhere."

"Maybe it was her door Mr. Stalker heard, sir," suggested Copper.

"Well, if it was, it's really rather irritating. I did ask specifically ..." Constable knocked again, and failing to get a reply, pushed open the door and marched into the room, Copper at his shoulder, only to stop dead in his tracks.

"Might as well put my book away for the

moment, sir," murmured Copper in a strained voice after a long pause. "I think our list just got one suspect shorter."

Chapter 13

Deborah Nye lay huddled on her side among the luxurious cushions of the room's four-poster bed. For one brief moment, Andy Constable had found himself hoping that the occupant was merely asleep, but even as he formulated the thought, he realised that the unnatural stillness had a quite different explanation.

The inspector moved towards the bed to take a closer look, and then turned swiftly to his junior. "Copper," he rapped out, "get Dr. Neal here double quick. Tell him to bring his bag. Then find Sheila Deare, wherever she is, and get her up here as well. Now!"

With a brief 'Sir!' of acknowledgement, Dave Copper sprinted off along the corridor in the direction of Perry Neal's room.

Constable approached the still and silent figure of the Justice Secretary and reached out a tentative finger to test for a pulse in the throat, hoping against hope that his first impression might be mistaken. As he did so, Dee's curtain of hair fell back, to reveal a hypodermic syringe buried up to the hilt in the side of the victim's neck. Constable let out a slow depressed-sounding sigh.

"Your sergeant said you wanted to see me urgently, inspector," came Perry Neal's voice from the doorway behind him. "Was there something ...?" The health minister's voice died away as he took in the scene before him.

"Please examine Mrs. Nye, doctor," replied Constable in a level voice. "As quickly as you can, if you will. She appears to be dead, but I may be mistaken. Perhaps there is something that can be done."

"Of course." Perry hurried to the bedside. He checked for a pulse. He lifted an eyelid. He reached into his bag for a stethoscope and listened intently, before stepping back with a deep sigh. "I'm sorry, inspector. She's gone. Only a matter of minutes this time, if I'm any judge, but I don't think there's anything to be done. But ..." He hesitated. "I don't understand. What's the syringe doing there? Is that something to do with you?"

"Not at all, sir," replied the inspector grimly. "But I think we may safely say that it has a great deal to do with Mrs. Nye's death. I wondered if perhaps you might have an explanation."

"Me? No. I mean, I carry syringes with me, but that isn't one of mine. Look." Perry burrowed in his bag and produced a package of hypodermics encased in their sterile wrappings. "See, the seal's intact. Anyway, this is a different type." He suddenly caught his breath. "Oh, for goodness sake, inspector, you don't think I had anything to do with this, do you?"

"I have to consider every possibility, sir." Constable refused to be swayed by the other's apparently horrified reaction. "Of all the people in the building, I can't at the moment think of anyone else likely to be in possession of such an item. So, would you have any thoughts on the possible cause of Mrs. Nye's death? Something's obviously been injected here. But what?"

Perry shook his head helplessly. "I couldn't say. Not without a proper examination. I mean, it's all too far out of my field."

The inspector gazed at the huddled figure in the bed for a few moments and then turned back to Perry. "Then I think there's nothing more you can do here to help me, doctor, so if you would be good enough to return to your room, I'd be grateful. Oh, and I'm sure I probably don't need to say this, but I shall expect you to keep this situation to yourself."

"Since you're keeping us all away from one another, inspector, that isn't going to be exactly difficult," replied Perry.

"As you say, sir." Constable regarded Perry steadily as the minister retrieved his bag and, with an awkward nod, turned and left the room, almost colliding with a somewhat breathless returning Dave Copper.

"Inspector Deare's on her way up, guv," he reported. "She was back in the kitchen."

"Did you tell her what's happened?"

"I thought I'd leave that job to you, sir," said Copper. "She was just coming off her phone to someone senior - I didn't like to ask exactly who - and she didn't look as if she could cope with very much more in the way of bad news."

"She's going to have to get used to it," retorted Constable grimly. "Right. On the subject of phones, you can dial our doc up on yours, and then hand it over, while you go and roust out Sergeant Singleton, who I assume is still checking over the Prime Minister's room next door. Tell her we've got another crime scene for her attention, and I'll break the glad tidings to the doc that his last day at work just got even more interesting."

"Andy," crackled the voice on the phone. "Getting a bit impatient, aren't we? I hope you aren't expecting any progress reports on your latest victim. My new guest hasn't even arrived yet – I gather the van's on its way as we speak."

"I'm sorry to say you're going to have to turn it around and get it back here, doctor," said Constable. "Fresh developments, I'm afraid."

"If they've forgotten something, I'll tan their hides," growled the doctor. "I haven't got time to waste. I've got a long and happy retirement to look forward to, once I've got you and your dead friends out of my hair."

Constable couldn't repress a humourless smile at the doctor's turn of phrase. "Sadly, that happy moment is going to have to be postponed a little longer, doctor. And you say 'latest victim'. If only that were the case."

"What are you talking about, man?"

"There's been another death."

"What!"

"And it's another murder. Mrs. Deborah Nye, the Justice Secretary, has been killed. Some kind of injection, by the look of it, but I need you to tell me what's involved."

The doctor sighed profoundly. "And I suppose I've got to clamber back into my car and come and take a look at the body?"

"I think I can spare you that at least, doc. I've got a doctor on the spot – the fact that he's also the Health Secretary may or may not be a bonus – and other than the fact that he's testifying that the lady's dead, I don't think there's much to be added. Plus we have someone from SOCO here, so with her report and photos, I'm hoping that you'll have enough to form your conclusions."

"Well, thank you for that, at least. Now, you'd better go away while I get on to the van driver and turn him round. I dare say you have more pressing things to do than talk to me."

"That, doctor, couldn't be more true."

"I'll be in touch." The line clicked off.

Constable became aware that Sheila Deare and Una Singleton were both standing just inside the door to the room, with Dave Copper hovering behind them. The SOCO sergeant was already intent on the recumbent form of Dee Nye, and at a nod from Constable, moved forward and began calmly to examine the body and its surroundings, while Sheila's face wore an expression of stunned bewilderment.

"I'm afraid, Sheila, that your day just got worse," said Constable.

The security officer seemed to be having difficulty containing her bemusement. "How can this have happened? I mean, who ...?"

"Your team of ministers is sheltering a

double killer," replied Constable shortly. "No other explanation. Unless we have a conspiracy with more than one perpetrator. Either way, it looks as if the late Prime Minister was not such a good picker of people as one would wish."

"So what on earth am I to do now?" Sheila still seemed at a loss.

Constable considered for a moment. "I think the only thing to do at this point is to get everyone together. At least, that way, we can stop this turning into an epidemic. Because obviously, my deciding to keep everyone apart has given someone the opportunity to break out and kill again. So, if you will, please collect everyone – Copper will help you – and gather them all together downstairs. The drawing room is probably best, if there's enough space."

"I'll get some extra chairs through from the dining room, guv," volunteered Copper.

"Do I tell them what's happened?" asked Sheila.

"I think not," said Constable. "I want to see their reactions when we break the news, so it's probably best if we can keep the element of surprise, as far as we can. Not that that will hold good for at least two of the company. Dr. Neal knows about Mrs. Nye – I got him in here to confirm that she was in fact dead. And, of course, whoever killed her."

"Unless they're one and the same person, of course, guv," pointed out Copper. "I can't think offhand of anyone who would know how to handle a syringe better than a doctor."

"Can't you?" replied Constable. He seemed momentarily distracted, as if a thought was hovering, just out of sight. "Well, be that as it may, if you and Inspector Deare would see to collecting everyone together, including Messrs Knightly and Daly. Sheila, I'd appreciate it if you'd stay with the group and keep them under your eye. I'll stay here and hear what Sergeant Singleton has to say."

"Righty-ho, guv." Copper stood back to allow Sheila to lead the way on their mission.

"Well, Singleton?" enquired Constable heavily. "What's the picture?"

"Here or elsewhere, sir?"

"Let's start with here."

"Not a lot I can say, sir. Yes, it's highly probable that this syringe, and whatever was in it, has been the cause of Mrs. Nye's death, but until it's removed, there's no way I can attempt any sort of analysis of what it contained, and I daren't tread on the doctor's toes by touching it. But I'll try to scan it for prints. There doesn't seem to be any evidence of a struggle, so I'm guessing that whatever happened was very quick and surprising and almost immediately successful in at least subduing the lady."

"No force? No evidence of violence?"

Una shook her head. "Not easy for me to tell, sir. There might be some marks which are the start of bruising round the mouth."

"As if a hand has been held over it? Is that what you mean?"

"Maybe, sir. It's not really my area of

expertise. But if you want an answer to the question I think you're asking, I don't think there would have been the need for any particular degree of strength."

"So not necessarily a man? Equally possibly a woman?"

"That's right, sir."

"Wonderful," grunted Constable. "Not exactly narrowing the field down, are we? So, what else do you have? I'm hoping that you've got something more positive to tell me about what you've found next door and downstairs."

"Just a few findings, sir," said Una. "I hope they'll be helpful." She cast an uneasy eye over the body. "Could we perhaps discuss them somewhere else, sir? It's not exactly conducive to conversation in here, is it?"

"You're right, of course, sergeant," said Constable. "We'll adjourn downstairs. I should imagine that Mr. Knightly's office may be free by now, so you can let me have your thoughts in comfort before you come back up here to do what you can while we wait for the body to be removed. I dare say you'll want to take a large number of photos and test whatever you can for fingerprints, and so on." He smiled sympathetically. "Probably more like your usual routine, I expect. You don't usually find yourself in at the kill, so to speak."

Una echoed his smile in a rather shakier version. "That's true, sir."

"Then let's be about it." The inspector ushered the SOCO officer from the room, closing the door behind him, and followed her down the stairs.

Seated in Phil Knightly's office, Constable looked at Una expectantly.

She drew a breath, pulled her tablet computer from her bag, opened it, and swiped the screen. "I'll start with the library, sir. There were two whisky glasses on the desk, both with remnants of liquid in them, which is most probably from the decanter nearby. I've bagged them, and I've also managed to take samples of the contents for analysis, but at a guess, considering that there's been no suggestion of poisoning, I'm not going to find anything untoward. But I do have some fingerprints. There's one set on both glasses, so that would most likely belong to the person who poured both drinks."

"Any identities?"

"Oh yes, sir. Fortunately. I was able to take a scan of Mrs. Ronson's prints ..."

"Oh yes. I remember that useful little scanner of yours from the case at the theatre."

"... and the ones on both glasses are hers. Plus another set on the other glass."

"So, hosting a little drinks party which we know nothing about. And the other prints?"

"Not so far identified, sir, but that's because I've not had a chance to go around everybody in the house. Will you want me to do that?"

"I think it's going to be essential, sergeant. We need to know who that other person was."

"One thing I can tell you, sir. Those other

prints are also on the plate of sandwiches which was on the desk."

"Just those?"

"Yes, sir."

"And the sandwiches are untouched. So," mused Constable, "we have someone coming to the library, at some time outside the programme of prime ministerial interviews with the ministers, and bringing a plate of provisions, for which the reward seems to have been a cosy drink and a chat. But who is the angel of mercy, I wonder? And did the chat lead on to more unpleasant consequences?" He pondered for a moment. "Get me those print results as soon as you can, please. So, moving on, what next?"

"Well, sir, you know about the napkin which we assumed came from the sandwich plate. I'm afraid I was right about the murder weapon – no fingerprints other than a couple of smudges, but the napkin has succeeded in erasing them pretty effectively. I've got the napkin bagged, and I'm sure there'll be DNA, but I'll be surprised if the blood on it turns out to be anything other than Mrs. Ronson's. As for the knife, you saw for yourself. It's very unusual. Silver, and it's a very modern design. I can't tell you where that came from."

"But as it happens, I can," remarked Constable. "According to the hotel manager, Mr. Knightly, it's his, and belongs with the rest of that set sitting on the desk just there." He pointed.

Una took a closer look. "Yes, sir. I can see identical design features."

"So if you had been able to find any prints on it, I have no doubt that they would have been Mr. Knightly's. Which, given his apparent lack of motive, does not advance us much."

"There's something else, sir," pointed out Una. "There's the other knife."

"Yes, I know. There was a paper-knife on the library desk, but as it was plainly sitting there innocuously, I didn't attach too much significance to it."

"No, not that one, sir," contradicted Una. "The other one."

"What other one?" enquired Constable, startled. "Where?"

"On that plate of sandwiches, sir. Just a very ordinary knife - it looks as if it came from a conventional cutlery service. I dare say if I check in the kitchen, I'll find its fellows, so I wouldn't expect to draw any conclusions from that. Except that, although it was to hand, it wasn't used in the murder. So I would guess that the murder weapon was taken from here to the library purposely."

"Hmmm," said Constable. "I missed that. Congratulations. You seem quite adept at making deductions from rather sketchy facts, sergeant. I'm impressed. Are you sure you didn't miss your vocation? I suspect you would make quite a formidable detective."

With a slight blush, Una hurried on. "That's about all I could get from downstairs, sir. I mean, there's plenty more, but I don't know how useful it would be to you. The door handle of the library is a mass of prints, as is the chair by the library desk, but I understand that everyone was in that room at some point because of all the meetings David ... Sergeant Copper told me about, so I don't know that there's anything to be gained by trying to identify them. And I can't see any real evidence that Mrs. Ronson's body had been moved since her death ... although ..."

"Although what?" enquired Constable sharply.

"Well ... there was something about the position of the head. It didn't look absolutely right to me. Not as it would lie naturally if the body had just fallen and stayed there."

"So what are you thinking?"

"I suppose it might just be that the person who found the body touched it to check whether the Prime Minister was actually dead, sir. That might account for it."

"Except that Mr. Knightly, who discovered Mrs. Ronson, claims that he didn't touch the body at all. So," reflected Constable, "if he didn't, who did?" He paused for a moment. "Anything else from downstairs?" Una shook her head. "In which case, we'll move upstairs. What about Mrs. Ronson's room?"

Una pulled a face. "Sorry, sir, but it's either a case of too little information, or too much. It's pretty clear that the room had been cleaned comprehensively, but I'm assuming that that was in anticipation of the Prime Minister's arrival. I've got her prints all over the bedroom and the bathroom – taps, wardrobe door-handles and the like – but virtually nothing else except a few partials. My guess would be that the chambermaid probably wore rubber gloves to do her work – there are some traces of the sort of powder they use inside those one-use gloves. Oh, and quite a number of Mrs. Ronson's prints around the desk and its chair, sir – it looks as if she spent some time seated there."

"I think we were already pretty sure of that, sergeant," said Constable. "There was the draft of a letter she had been writing left in the waste-bin. It's up there on the desk."

"I saw it, sir. But – I hope I didn't overstep any bounds – I also took a look at the P.M.'s briefcase, as it was lying there open. I thought you'd want to know if it had been handled by anyone unauthorised."

"Apart from me, you mean?" enquired the inspector with grim humour. "And ..."

"Mrs. Ronson's prints all over the outside, sir. Plus another set, which I might be able to identify if ..." She looked at Constable hesitantly.

"If ...?" Constable caught on. "All right, sergeant. Produce your little machine, and let's see if we can eliminate me. Funny," he remarked, as Una busied herself with her equipment, "I'm not sure I've ever been fingerprinted before. Apart from at the gates of an American theme park, that is, but that's another story. Interesting to have a new experience at this stage in my career." A bleep seemed to indicate the arrival of a result.

"Yes, overwhelmingly you, sir," said Una

with what sounded like relief. "The contents of the case are another matter. A mass of prints all over the folders of government papers, but I suppose you'd expect that. And I noticed the hotel's register, which seemed rather an odd thing to be there, so I took a look at that, but as you'd expect, it's got prints all over it from goodness knows how many people."

"It's more the contents of that which interest me," replied Constable. "I want to find out what Mrs. Ronson was expecting to learn from it, so that's on Copper's list of to-dos. Anything else?"

"No, sir. That's about it so far."

"Then I suggest," said Constable, getting to his feet and stretching, "that we go and find your ... go and find Copper, check that he's marshalled all our suspects in one place, and you can get on with fingerprinting them while I set him about other tasks. Let's see what's afoot in the drawing room."

Chapter 14

The faces which turned to greet Andy Constable as he passed through the door of the drawing room wore expressions which ranged from weary to wary, with variations of impatience and resignation along the way.

After a momentary pause and a brief survey of her fellow ministers, Amanda Laye appeared to elect herself spokesman, and advanced towards the detective with determined steps. "Inspector Constable," she challenged, "your superiors will most certainly be hearing from me over this completely unacceptable situation. My colleagues and I have been kept under virtual lock and key while being subjected to what amounts to an unwarranted inquisition, and then we are brought here, by your orders, I gather, by police personnel who appear to be under some vow of silence. I think you may be in danger of forgetting who you are dealing with. I warn you, inspector, the consequences of your actions could be very serious indeed."

"Miss Laye," returned the inspector mildly, "I think you need not remind me of the seriousness of the situation. In fact, it has become more serious than you realise – most of you, that is."

Amanda frowned. "What on earth do you mean, inspector? Are you saying that you have identified the person who was responsible for killing the Prime Minister?"

"As yet, no," admitted Constable.

"Then what are you saying? Why do you speak of most of us?" The Foreign Secretary looked around the room. "And why isn't Deborah Nye here? Are you holding her separately?"

"I'm afraid the absence of Mrs. Nye is the reason why I say that the situation has become more serious," replied Constable, "and also why I have had you all gathered together here. No, we are not holding Mrs. Nye – I regret to say that she too has been killed."

There was an immediate intake of breath from around the room, followed by a shocked silence.

Lewis Stalker was the first to find his voice. "What, murdered? But ... where? Was it up in her room?"

A nod from Constable. "I'm very much afraid so, sir."

"And you think ... that it was one of us?"

"There can be no other explanation, Mr. Stalker."

"So somebody went in there ... I mean, I said I heard a door ... Oh my god." Lew subsided, apparently stunned.

"And therefore, ladies and gentlemen," resumed Constable, "I have to ask for your further co-operation. There are certain items at the scenes of both deaths which may be relevant to our enquiries. Sergeant Singleton here," he indicated the young woman standing behind him, "is an experienced Scene Of Crime Officer, and she will be taking scans of your fingerprints.

With your permission, naturally. And largely for elimination purposes, of course." He gazed around the assembly as if challenging any of those present to object, and then turned to Sheila Deare, who had been seated unobtrusively in a corner of the room. "Inspector Deare, perhaps you would be kind enough to oversee the process. And perhaps you would send Singleton to report to me in Mr. Knightly's office when she's finished." He turned away. "Discreetly, if you please, sergeant," he added in an undertone to Una. "Whatever you happen to find by way of matching prints, please keep it to yourself until you've spoken to me. No give-away reactions."

"Understood, sir." Una began to unpack the equipment from her case.

"Mr. Knightly!"

"Yes, inspector?" Phil looked up from his position seated at the bureau by the window.

"I shall be wanting to use the computer in your office. I hope that will present no problem."

"No, of course not, inspector. Except that it's password-protected."

"Then I shall be needing your password, sir, if you'd be good enough to jot it down for me," insisted Constable firmly. "But you can rest assured, it will go no further."

"Oh. All right." Phil took a sheet of paper from the desk and swiftly wrote the required details.

After a brief glance at the paper and a small smile, Constable turned to his junior colleague. "Sergeant Copper!"

"Sir?" Dave Copper came smartly to attention from where he had been leaning alongside the fireplace.

"We shall leave the ladies to their task. You're with me." Constable led the way back out into the hall. "Well, at least there's one further possibility eliminated."

"What's that, guv?"

"The writing on the mysterious note about the infiltrator. It doesn't match Mr. Knightly's, so at least we can be sure he wasn't the author. I'm not sure what that tells us, but every little helps."

Copper peered over his superior's shoulder at the few jotted letters and symbols and shrugged. "So now what, guv?"

"I want you to retrieve the hotel register from Mrs. Ronson's room and go through it line by line. There's something in there, and I want to know what it is."

"On my way sir." Copper started up the stairs. "I'll come and find you in the office."

"No," ordered Constable. "I want some quiet time on my own. Let me have your notebook to peruse, and then you can go and ensconce yourself in the library, now that Singleton has finished in there."

"Very good, sir. I'll let you know if I turn up anything." Copper handed over his notebook, now becoming rather battered, and disappeared in the direction of the Chinese Bedroom.

Constable opened the door, almost undetectable in the hall's wood panelling, which led to Philip Knightly's office and settled himself behind the desk. He closed his eyes for a moment and drank in the precious silence. Time to take stock.

How on earth, he wondered, did this situation come about in the first place? What could have prompted a prime minister, still relatively new in the job, to call together a seemingly disparate group of her cabinet ministers in an unusually secretive manner? Mention had been made of a possible pending government re-shuffle. Perhaps some of the ministers were in their positions more through inertia than choice – maybe some of them had been kept on in their former jobs under the old government in the interests of continuity, but Mrs. Ronson had decided that this was not an acceptable arrangement for the long term. Constable didn't feel himself to be sufficiently well-informed regarding the political ins and outs of the previous few months to judge. So, simply a show of strength by the new broom at Number 10? And why the cloak-and-dagger scenario? Prime ministers were surely more notorious for wielding the axe in a highly visible manner when rearranging their team.

The other question was, why this specific group of individuals? Constable felt he knew the answer here. It was evident that, at some stage since the group had arrived in Dammett Worthy, Mrs. Ronson had exchanged words with each of the suspects which pointed to a cause for friction. Each of the ministers had found themselves the target of critical remarks. And no doubt those criticisms, sadly only hinted at though disjointed pieces of conversation overheard by various witnesses, would have been given full rein in the private interviews to which the Prime Minister had summoned each of her colleagues. Oh, to have been a fly on the wall during those meetings, mused the inspector. One of them must have contained revelations so damaging, so dangerous, that the person at the receiving end had tipped over the edge into murder. Because the Prime Minister had absolute power over who held office and who did not. The fate of each person was in her hands, and hers alone. Remove her, and you may well remove any threat to yourself. So, he thought, let's see what we can glean from what we've been told. He opened Copper's notebook and began to survey the sergeant's cramped notes.

Among the ministers, Deborah Nye had been the first to be subjected to the detectives' attentions. Well, thought Constable ruefully, at least we can dismiss her from our list of suspects. Her own death would seem to rule her out as a likely culprit. Unless ... Constable's train of thought came to a sudden halt. Unless the killing of Deborah Nye was carried out because she had been responsible for the murder of the Prime Minister, and Mrs. Nye's own death was some sort of punishment or revenge carried out by ... whom? An ardent supporter of Mrs. Ronson who had discovered the truth, and visited their own form of justice on the Justice Secretary? Constable groaned inwardly. Surely this was a fantastical scenario too far. But then why should Mrs. Nye herself be killed? First things first, thought the inspector. What might have been the cause of conflict between Deborah and her superior, sufficient to present a serious enough threat to her position to warrant a violent remedy?

Andy Constable leafed back through Dave Copper's notes. There seemed to be precious little data to go on. A discussion, overheard by Phil Knightly, between Deborah Nye and Marion Hayste prior to the group's departure to the Dammett Well Inn for dinner, which didn't really point to anything to Mrs. Nye's detriment. Other remarks, half caught by Lena Cross while she was waiting at table, where the minister had been involved in an exchange regarding massaged academic statistics. There had been mention of fraud and families, but again, the references were too vague to point in a specific direction, and could have been directed towards any of the participants in that discussion. But ... Constable called to mind the draft letter which Doris Ronson had been composing in her room, but which she had then discarded. Could this be a pointer to reservations on the Prime Minister's part about Mrs. Nye's position? Who would need to be 'above suspicion' more than the Justice Secretary? Was there something in her past which jeopardised her standing? Hadn't Jim Daly expressed reservations about her husband's character?

The next interviewee had been Milo Grade.

A distant acquaintance of Philip Knightly's, according to the hotel manager, although the minister insisted that he had no recollection of it. Well, which of us can be expected to remember everyone whose path we've crossed during our years of education, mused Constable reasonably. But education was Mr. Grade's portfolio, and he appeared to have more significant issues to deal with. Back to the academic statistics. If there were fraud being perpetrated in the exam results figures, to what extent could Milo be held responsible, if that were the point at issue? Certainly the exchanges over dinner pointed in that direction, despite Milo's assertion that shop-talk during the meal had been banned. Very much the reverse, it appeared. Constable consulted his junior's notebook once again. Yes, there had been a brief clash between Milo Grade and Dee Nye in which the Prime Minister was involved. Could that have caused some sort of animus against Dee on the part of Milo? Enough to give him a motivation to kill her? It sounded far-fetched. Especially if, as seemed possible, the failings at Milo's ministry, the Education Department, were in place before he assumed his position. Surely there wouldn't be enough jeopardy there for him to fear dismissal by Mrs. Ronson. And therefore, why kill her?

Constable turned another dog-eared page to arrive at Copper's notes on the subject of Amanda Laye. He winced slightly. A formidable woman, not to be trifled with. And certainly one who would not take kindly to unjustifiable accusations. But Mrs. Ronson seemed to have been in no awe of her forceful colleague. She'd referred several times to Miss Laye's activities, both before and during her tenure at the Foreign Office, including a remark Phil Knightly had overheard. There seemed to have been an unaccountably large number of references to affairs in the Middle East, despite the fact that Amanda's most recent trip had not involved a visit to that area. Constable was disinclined to put too much credence in the lady's attempt to fob off an overheard mention of the Gulf as merely part of someone's turn of phrase. The coincidence was too much to ignore. Constable furrowed his brow. Hadn't Seamus Daly mentioned one of the local rulers? And someone had been said to be up in arms over something. Was it Mrs. Ronson herself, who disapproved of some aspect of Miss Laye's activities? But to anyone who took even the slightest passing interest in politics, it was surely no news that the Foreign Office and Downing Street often had wildly differing views over the country's place in the world and where its best interests lay. Where was the motive for murder there? And how could the death of Deborah Nye be drawn into the mix? Some legal aspect of the Foreign Secretary's activities which stood at odds with her continuation in the job?

With a small sigh, the inspector moved on to Copper's jottings relating to Lewis Stalker. Another who'd referred to the intended moratorium on political discussions at the dinner table, and another who'd scoffed at the idea as fatuous when it came to the event. Hardly surprising in Mr. Stalker's case, reflected Constable. The Media Secretary came across as the most open-hearted, open-faced individual of all the ministers present. Ideal perhaps in the context of his position dealing with the press and television, but perhaps therein lay the dangers. Too open? Too ready with an opinion? Certainly he seemed to have been taken to task at one point by Mrs. Ronson, who had spoken of him guarding his tongue, according to the evidence of Jim Daly. Lew may have come back with what sounded like a flippant retort, but then Dee Nye had been drawn into the conversation, also in a critical vein, so perhaps there had been a sharper edge to the exchange than appeared on the surface. Was the veneer of good humour a disguise for something far more serious? Certainly 'indefensible' was quite a strong word for the Prime Minister to use in relation to the public behaviour of one of her colleagues. Constable strained to remember the words used in Daly's account of the scene. What had been the context? Suddenly, with a rueful smile, he metaphorically smote his forehead. Dolt! He surely already had the information in his hands. Or at least, in his pocket. He fished out the computer stick retrieved from Doris Ronson's briefcase and looked at the words written on it. 'The Nightly Politics - that interview'. Was the explanation really that obvious? Constable swiftly lifted the lid of the laptop on the desk in front of him, typed in the requisite codes, inserted the USB stick and, after a tentative foray through the menu, found what he was looking for. He pressed the enter key, and sat back as the opening credits of a television programme began to roll.

Some minutes later, Constable closed the laptop and turned his attention back to Dave Copper's notebook. Next to be featured was Marion Hayste, the Prisons Minister. The only member of what might be called the second rank of ministers to be included in the proceedings, observed Constable. All the other participants in the gathering were at the very forefront of government activity. Was there any significance in this? Or was it simply because, as Marion and her ministerial superior Dee Nye had indicated, there was a particular policy initiative in hand, and this was a topic which needed to be discussed sooner rather than later? The two women had both been fairly dismissive and non-committal on the subject when interviewed, but Jim Daly had an inkling that the policy might have related to drugs, and Marion herself had admitted the fact during her second conversation with the detectives. And Phil Knightly had walked in on a conversation between the ministers from the Justice Department which pointed to the fact that not all minds were at one on the subject. But how could this have translated into a threat to the Prime Minster?

There was another fact which jarred slightly – what precisely was the relationship between Marion Hayste and Perry Neal? If indeed there was such a thing. Perry had certainly said nothing to indicate any relationship beyond the purely professional, but Marion had been surprisingly quick in her denials of anything over and above that. Too quick? She had been flustered in her account of the final stages of the interviews with Mrs. Ronson, when she and the Health Secretary had been left alone, the last two to be called in. And her statement that she had never been into Dr. Neal's room had been swift and emphatic. Could it possibly be that, given the difference in their ages and despite the stolidly conventional doctor's lack of obvious attractiveness to a vivacious young woman, there was a connection between the widower and the married woman? Such stories are famously grist to the mill of the media. Might Doris Ronson have got wind of any affair? Scandals in the early life of a government are always best avoided, and could the best way to suppress such revelations be to dismiss one or both of the persons involved?

Which brought Constable's thoughts neatly to the subject of Perry Neal himself. As the inspector considered the mature former G.P., he reflected on the implausibility of the theory he had spent the last few moments creating. Surely, had there been anything to uncover in that area, Jim Daly's reporter's instincts would have seized on it in very short order. And as he himself had said, he had next to no information in his own dossier on the Health Secretary. Abandoning his previous thoughts, Constable leafed through Copper's notes from the detectives' conversation with Dammett Worthy's vicar. Here was clear and positive evidence of an interaction between Doris Ronson and Perry Neal which the latter had certainly found uncomfortable. There had been talk concerning a tragic case in his past, which seemed to have unaccountably moved him. The Prime Minister had spoken of praying for the forgiveness of sins, and Perry's reaction had been to insist that his efforts were concentrated so that such tragedies could not occur in the future. But how effective were his efforts proving? Was he called to this meeting to be taken to task for his failures to improve matters in the Health Service? Did these sins relate to the work of his ministry, or did they have something to do with his life before he came into politics?

The exquisite Erica Mayall was the next subject of Dave Copper's copious note-taking. Andy Constable allowed himself a small moment of sympathy for the strains put on his junior colleague's skills as a minute-taker. And there had been plenty of revelations to record, largely from Erica herself. But then, she'd had little choice. There had been numerous references heard by several people which related to the minister's perceived extravagance in her expenditure, with pointed remarks about shoes being cited as an indication of discord between the Prime Minister and her ... Constable found himself slightly at a loss to decide on the correct term to describe the relationship between Doris Ronson and her colleague. Friends certainly, even extremely close friends, with a mutual attraction which Erica insisted had never stepped beyond the pure and platonic. Not that there would necessarily have been any cause for concern there, even if that were not quite true. In these days, reflected the inspector, there are so many figures in public life who are entirely content that all aspects of their private lives and personalities should be an open book, that any personal revelations about the two women would probably have caused scarcely more than a temporary ripple in the media. Perhaps even sympathy and understanding. On the other hand, politicians received a very hard press if they were found to be abusing their position in financial terms. Taxes and expenses were extremely toxic subjects, and the Prime Minister's despatch box had contained a report on the subject from a very powerful parliamentary committee. So might Erica have put herself in jeopardy over her finances, which would have left Doris Ronson with no choice but to sacrifice the minister to protect herself? Leading, thought Constable wryly, to the act rebounding on the Prime Minister in the most drastic way imaginable? Which left unanswered the question of the mysterious 'Heather'. Were the inspector's closing surmises during his final interview with Erica uncomfortably close to the truth? The words 'Hell hath' rose unbidden in his mind once more.

With a slight sigh of relief that he was coming to the end of his list, Constable turned to the jottings which related to Benjamin Fitt. On the surface, a bluff man-of-the-people character, who had come into politics from a very different background and by a very different route from the majority of his colleagues. Did this set him apart in some way? Did it make him feel like an outsider? And if so, could that provide any plausible reason why he should resort to the murder of one or more of his colleagues? The inspector surveyed the evidence before him. Jim Daly seemed to have a feeling that there was something to uncover, on the basis of whispers he had heard going around Whitehall, but there was no firm basis for suspicion. Milo Grade, however, had heard an exchange between Mrs. Ronson and Benny in the car on the way to the Dammett Well which sounded as if it had left him uneasy but, perhaps because of the presence of others in the car, the conversation had not developed further. On the other hand, when the party had been leaving the Inn, the Prime Minister had tackled the Social Security Minister once more, again on the subject of families, and Gideon Porter had heard her make reference to what sounded like a specific case in the area where he had been brought up. She was firmly intending to pursue the matter further. So was there some dangerous skeleton lurking in Benny's past which might have cut his feet from under him in his ministerial position? But even so, thought Constable, that wouldn't account for the killing of Deborah Nye. Unless the potential scandal had some legal aspect which had not so far been revealed.

With a deep sigh, the inspector closed the notebook, leaned back in the chair, and shut his eyes. Slowly, painstakingly, he allowed the thoughts to shuffle around in his brain like the pieces of a jigsaw puzzle, turning over the blanks, rejecting those which did not seem to form part of a pattern, and allowing those to remain in place which appeared to belong together. Around him, the house seemed to be waiting in hushed anticipation, with only the tiniest sounds to be heard. The slight occasional tick from the pipes of the central heating system as a fresh pulse of hot water moved around the circuit. An infinitesimal creak of timber as the house breathed. After a while in this contemplative state, Constable was roused to full alertness by a hesitant tap at the door.

"Yes? What is it?"

The door to the hall opened, and the head of Una Singleton appeared. "Sorry to interrupt you, sir. David ... Sergeant Copper told me that you were going over things quietly by yourself and wouldn't want to be disturbed, but I thought you'd like to know that I've finished that job you asked me to do, and I've got some results for you."

"That's perfectly all right, sergeant," replied Constable. "In fact, I'm glad you're here. I was hoping for a few extra pieces to help me complete the picture, and you may well be able to provide them."

"David said that he's got some more information for you too, sir. He's still in the library. Do you want me to go and fetch him?"

"No, I think we'll go and join him there," said Constable, uncoiling himself from his chair. "I suspect the three of us would be more comfortable in there, rather than squashed in here." He gathered up the items before him. "So lead on, and we'll hear what you've both got to say."

In the library, Dave Copper was to be found seated at the library desk, its top spread with books and papers. He looked up, his face bearing a satisfied smile. "How are we doing, guv?"

"By the look of you, you seem to be doing well. I assume you're happy with your researches?"

"Very much so, sir. I've been through the hotel register, and I think you'll be interested in what I've found out there. I also took the liberty of taking that report on expenses that was in Mrs. Ronson's briefcase, just on the off-chance there might be something squirrelled away in it, and I've got a little snippet for you from that. And also, I think I've solved the puzzle of the mysterious Heather."

"Sounds good," said Constable. "Do you think you've done as well, Singleton?"

"I hope so, sir. I've got all the fingerprints you wanted. And David had a suggestion, which I acted on. I got everyone to give me a sample of their hand-writing."

"Very resourceful," nodded Constable in approval. He settled into a large leather armchair. "You two have been busy. Well, you'd better let me have what you've got."

Chapter 15

"Yes, sir. I understand completely." Sheila Deare's voice echoed around the hall as the team of police officers emerged from the library. "Yes, sir. I will make sure that he is in no doubt that time is pressing." She eyed the grandfather clock standing alongside her. "As soon as that, sir? Very well. I will tell him ... Yes, sir, that's clear ... Yes. Goodbye." She ended the call and turned to face the new arrivals.

"Pressure from above, inspector?" enquired Andy Constable.

"You might say that, Andy," responded Sheila grimly. "That was the Deputy P.M. He's growing increasingly impatient, and he's worried that he won't be able to keep the lid on this situation very much longer. Apparently there are already murmurs drifting around Whitehall, wondering where everybody is and why they can't be contacted. I ... we ... you've been given a deadline."

Constable raised his eyebrows. "And that is ...?"

"Three-quarters of an hour. If I don't get back in touch with Downing Street by the top of the hour, the Deputy P.M. says he's going to have no choice but to go public."

"With everything? Including the death of Mrs. Nye?"

Sheila closed her eyes in despair. "Please don't remind me, Andy. He was incandescent, to say the least. I've had it pointed out to me in no uncertain terms that security means security, and in the absence of it, I should be feeling none too secure myself. I think I'm due for a very uncomfortable conversation when I get back to London."

Constable looked at his watch. "Top of the hour? In that case, I think we ought to get on with it, don't you? Your three-quarters of an hour has already turned into forty-four minutes."

"What? You mean ... you've got the answer?"

"I have an answer," Constable corrected her gently. "I'm very much hoping it's the right one. So, shall we?" He turned the handle of the door to the drawing room and led his colleagues inside. He advanced to the centre of the room, while the other officers ranged themselves along the wall by the door.

Unease was palpable throughout the group seated around the room. After a glance at her fellow ministers, none of whom seemed disposed to speak, Amanda Laye once again took the initiative and rose. "Inspector Constable, I have to insist that this situation is brought to an end."

"Then I'm very happy to be able to fall in with your wishes, Foreign Secretary," replied Constable smoothly. "That is precisely why I am here. Nothing will please me more than to be able to release you – most of you – so that you can resume your ministerial duties." While you still have them, he thought to himself.

"You mean you've identified the person

who killed the Prime Minister?" Amanda once again looked around those present. "Well," she demanded, "who?"

Without answering, Constable moved to take up a position at the fireplace where he could survey everyone in the room. All eyes followed him.

"This entire case has revolved around the matter of secrets and revelations," he began. "The first question which needed to be answered was, why did Mrs. Ronson call this particular group of her colleagues together and exclude others? The answer gradually emerged – it was because each person here was carrying uncomfortable truths from their past or present which, in one way or another, made them vulnerable in the office they hold.

"I should perhaps digress here, because not every one of you falls into that category. Mr. Knightly, I'm confident that you are in no way responsible for what has occurred in your hotel over the past day or so. But having said that, in a way, your presence, or absence, has been more critical than you know. But I will come on to that later.

"And then, of course, we have Mr. Daly. You also, I'm quite sure, can be absolved completely from any involvement in the death of Mrs. Ronson. Your alibi is as sound as it could possibly be. You were away from the premises, in the company of the P.M.'s security officer. And because the murder of Deborah Nye is linked in with that of the late Prime Minister, I am content to rule you out there also. Of course, that's not to say you don't have secrets of your own. In fact, you would scarcely have been able to carry out your most recent assignment if you didn't."

"What are you talking about, secrets?" enquired Amanda sharply. "The man's a waiter. What possible secrets could he have that would affect what's gone on here?"

"His secret, Miss Laye," replied Constable, "is that he was on a mission to discover yours." Puzzled looks were exchanged around the room. "I have to tell you that the man you know as Jim Daly, a member of the catering staff at Number 10, whom you probably scarcely acknowledge in your routine activities, is in fact better known as Seamus Daly. He is an investigative reporter on a tabloid newspaper, and he had inveigled his way into the Number 10 staff in pursuit of a story about the inner machinations of government."

A variety of expressions of horror was etched on the faces of all the ministers as they turned to gaze at the reporter.

Jim gave a candid grin and held up his hands in mock surrender. "Guilty as charged, I'm afraid, everyone. Living proof of the old adage that you've all got two ears and one mouth for a reason, and that you should always listen twice as much as you speak. Not that I'm not grateful to you all for the loose talk – the amount I've learnt ever since I joined the staff has given me enough material for a very nice little book deal when all this is over."

"But ... surely he'll have signed something

when he was taken on," spluttered Lew Stalker in indignation, appealing to the room. "Official Secrets Act or something. Wouldn't he be breaking the law?"

"I'm afraid I'm not in a position to answer that, Mr. Stalker," said Constable. "And since the lady who might have been able to provide an opinion is no longer with us, we shall have to leave the question of Mr. Daly's legal situation to one side. But as you raise it, let's consider the question of official secrets for a moment. In some cases, revealing them is a crime. People go to prison. But in other cases, information which the government would rather keep under wraps can slip out as a result of simple irresponsibility. People have been photographed carrying confidential official papers in plain view as they walk up Downing Street. A person might be overheard while chatting to a colleague in a bar. Or someone might, perhaps almost in a display of showing-off, reveal details of government policy during an unguarded conversation. For example, in a television interview. And consider the likely consequences if a prime minister discovered that one of her team had done just that."

Lew squirmed. "I can't see that this has anything to do with me."

"You may as well not trouble to deny the facts, Mr. Stalker," said Constable. "Because among the Prime Minister's possessions, we found a computer stick with a recording on it. It was labelled 'That interview', which was already starting to sound a little ominous. I've played the recording, and it is indeed an interview. You, on a late-night television political show on one of the more obscure channels, talking about some perfectly anodyne story relating to your own department. But at the end, in response to a completely throw-away remark by the interviewer, you launched into a discussion of some plans which you had evidently heard about, regarding cuts in the British defence forces. Gold to the interviewer – you could tell from the expression on her face that she couldn't believe her luck, and she teased out more information from you than she could ever have hoped for. And, of course, the story reached the Prime Ministerial ear. Quite how she came by the recording we don't know – maybe it passed into her possession from some helpful but anonymous source – a senior ministerial colleague, perhaps. Suffice to say that it's clear that Mrs. Ronson took an extremely dim view of the matter – 'indefensible' was the word she was heard to use - and that your career was in the gravest jeopardy."

"If I'd ever found out who gave her that story ...," muttered Lew.

"Perhaps you did," said Constable. "Perhaps you discovered that it was Deborah Nye who had made you her target. And perhaps you took your revenge on her for what she had done to you." Lew simply gawped at the inspector, his mouth moving but no words emerging. "There's another candidate, of course, for letting your indiscretions be known. I just wondered if you might, in your movements among the media, have crossed paths with Seamus Daly. Maybe not closely, but perhaps he rang a bell with you. Did you half-recognise him? Did you pick up a hint that he knew what you had done? A simple look during the dinner at the Inn might have been enough. Perhaps you thought he might have put you in danger, and so you took steps to undermine his credibility."

"And how would I do that, inspector?" bluffed Lew.

"By the simple expedient of writing Mrs. Ronson an anonymous note," retorted Constable calmly. "Warning her that someone was not what they seemed. And therefore that what they might have provided to her was not to be relied upon. We've seen that note – the handwriting is yours, although there's been a feeble attempt to disguise it. It's not obvious what the note relates to. A distraction technique – spreading uncertainty. But the evidence of the recording was, unfortunately for you, irrefutable. As you yourself said to me, you were always told that your mouth would get you into trouble."

"Where is all this leading, inspector?" intervened Amanda Laye. "Are you telling us that Lewis had been responsible for these two murders?"

"By no means, Miss Laye," said Constable. "I'm merely pointing out that his motive is as good as that of many others. Yours, for instance."

"What?" Amanda sounded outraged. "Do you mean to say that you have concocted some fanciful notion that I could be responsible for what's gone on here?"

"Not fanciful, Miss Laye," said Constable. "I believe I can advance a perfectly plausible case for why you should have felt yourself to be in a dangerous position. Would you like me to do so?" A light of alarm flared in Amanda's eyes, and she resumed her seat, hands clasped tightly together in her lap. "Once again, I have to touch on the matter of defence," continued the inspector. "Oh, not of this country, but of one of our allies."

"Can I remind you, inspector, that I am not responsible for defence matters," pointed out Amanda coldly. "Foreign affairs are my concern. As witness the visit overseas from which I have just returned."

"Ah. Foreign affairs. Of course. But it's not your most recent trip which I think was of most concern to Mrs. Ronson. I have a suspicion, bolstered by some information which I've received during my conversations today, that it's foreign affairs of a more historic nature which were worrying the Prime Minister. Affairs of the heart. Because I understand that, in your youth, you became ... let's say extremely friendly with another student, who came from the Gulf area. Nothing wrong with that, of course – didn't someone once say that love is the prerogative of the young? But when, in the fullness of time, the young woman becomes an extremely important cabinet minister, and her lover becomes the ruler of a highly strategic ally, eyebrows might be raised over the nature of any continuing relationship. Certainly Mrs. Ronson was heard to comment – somebody thought they caught a remark about being 'up in arms'. But what if they'd misheard? I have to confess to a huge leap of guesswork here, but isn't it possible that the subject referred to was, in fact, 'supplying arms'? That part of the world is highly volatile. There are no doubt stringent regulations regarding the supply of weaponry. But what if someone were attempting to trade on old relationships in order to circumvent those strictures? That would be a very serious matter – quite possibly illegal. Might not a Prime Minister seek an opinion on that from her highest legal authority? And so you can see, Miss Laye, how a case could perfectly well be constructed as to why you might have found yourself in a threatened position, and why you might have pursued a violent solution."

"You're completely mad," said Amanda defiantly. "If you are seriously suggesting that I might have ... words fail me." She glared at the inspector.

"I am merely drawing a potential conclusion from the facts in my possession, Miss Laye," replied Constable.

"Well, then, I suppose you're going to do the same for all of us and lay everything bare," said Erica Mayall. The others in the room turned to regard her, surprised at the intervention. "Since you've been snooping into everyone's private life."

"Not snooping, I hope, Ms Mayall," said Constable. "Investigating, certainly. But in the course of that process, it's inevitable that certain facts will emerge which some people would prefer remained confidential."

Erica drew herself up. "Say what you must, inspector. I'm not afraid."

Constable gave a half-smile. "My compliments on your resolve, Ms. Mayall. Whatever emerges. Let me begin with what I'm sure many people here will have been aware of, since they were witnesses to some of the remarks passed by Mrs. Ronson over dinner. We kept hearing mention of shoes. An innocuous enough topic, but it turned into a critique of possible extravagance. There were hints of misuse of public funds, overseas trips which might have been seen as an excuse for self-indulgence under the guise of ministerial activity. Could such charges really be serious enough to warrant your dismissal? Quite possibly, it appeared, if they were backed up by a damning report by a parliamentary watchdog. As, we discover, they were. Because the Prime Minister had, among her papers, a copy of a report which provided evidence that such abuse of office had taken place. My colleague Sergeant Copper, having read some of that report, tells me that it sounds as if your career could not have been saved. Despite whatever Mrs. Ronson may have wished privately."

"Why 'privately', Mr. Constable?" queried Amanda. "If you're amassing all these theories regarding our supposed failings which would have set the Prime Minister against us, what would private wishes have had to do with anything? I thought you were saying that her duty would have been to dismiss us, and that's why we would have killed her. Preposterous though that sounds."

"There were other considerations in this instance," responded Constable, unruffled by Amanda's hostility. "And it sounds as if, close colleagues though all of you might have been, you may not have been particularly observant. It probably took an outsider – someone like Mr. Daly, for instance – to see the full picture."

"How is Daly involved?" asked Amanda, perplexed. She turned to the reporter. "Well?"

Jim gazed at the Foreign Secretary for a moment, and seemed to come to a conclusion. "I think," he said, "under the circumstances, this is one story I'm not going to break. I believe Erica has the right to tell it for herself." He shrugged. "If it's even a story these days."

Constable regarded the journalist with eyes in which could be seen a growing respect. "Mr. Daly, I confess you surprise me. I think you're right." He turned back to Erica. "Well, Ms Mayall, I don't know how much you wish to volunteer?"

"Doris and I loved each other," said Erica calmly. The ensuing silence lasted several long seconds, while all present studiously avoided any reaction. "And before anyone draws any conclusions from that," she continued, "it simply means that we had the dearest, closest, ... sweetest friendship anyone could ever have wished for. We cared for each other deeply and

... that's it. Nothing beyond that, in case some of you are making assumptions. We talked a lot, sometimes late into the night. She felt that she could tell me things that she couldn't share with anyone else. I've never known a relationship like it. And I don't suppose I ever will."

"And I believe you may even have had private names for one another, didn't you?" intervened Constable quietly.

Erica looked surprised. "Yes. Silly, I know. It was just our little whimsy. But ... how did you know?"

"We found a note," explained the inspector. "Rather personal in tone. It was signed 'Heather'. Which puzzled us for a while and sent us off on a wrong tangent, until my colleague Sergeant Copper, inspired by Mr. Daly's mother, did a little research. Sergeant?"

Copper stepped forward as everyone's attention became focussed on him. "It was nothing really. It's just that Mr. Daly had mentioned his mother's fondness for gardening, so I took a look in one of the reference books in the library, all about plants. And the official Latin name for heather is Erica."

"We could leave notes on one another's desks when we shared an office and nobody would know who had sent them," said Erica. She sighed. "I know. It makes us sound like a pair of silly schoolgirls with a crush."

"Although I'm still not sure about the way the note was addressed, sir ..." resumed Copper.

Erica coloured slightly. "It's a reference

from Greek mythology, sergeant," she broke in. "The character of Doris was one of the sea-nymphs."

"Ah," said Constable, "then I think we can leave it there." He signalled to his junior to resume his place.

"So there you are, inspector," said Erica. "Now you know everything."

"Not quite everything, Ms. Mayall," countered Constable. "I don't think you've told me quite all. You mentioned talking things over with Mrs. Ronson, late into the night. I think that's what may have happened here yesterday evening. There was a hint from one of your colleagues that the Prime Minister may have been waiting for someone after all the interviews in the library were finished. Someone with whom she could perhaps unburden some of the difficult decisions she was going to have to make. Someone who, perhaps, came bringing comfort in the form of a plate of sandwiches, and who shared a drink with her. Well ... am I right?"

Erica regarded him with amazement. "But ... how do you know all this?"

"Nothing particularly complicated, Ms. Mayall," smiled Constable. "Fingerprints on the glasses ... fingerprints on the sandwich plate ... it didn't take a miracle of detection."

"We talked," sighed Erica. "Well, she talked, and I listened. I offered to help her think things through, but she said her head was buzzing too much, so I left her alone. I went back up to my room. And that was the last time I saw her." She gazed around defiantly at her ministerial colleagues. "So if anyone is thinking that I might have taken the chance to harm her ..." Erica broke off and bit her lip in an effort to control her emotion. "Then you couldn't be more wrong."

"I agree," said Constable. "I think the fact that you made no efforts to remove the traces of your presence is a clear indication that you had nothing to conceal. You may not have told the full truth, but I don't put a sinister interpretation on that." He paused for a moment. "Of course, you weren't the only person not to have been completely candid about their movements." He suddenly directed his attention towards the Health Secretary. "Was she, Dr. Neal?"

"Me?" The astonishment was evident in Perry's voice. "What, you mean ...? Oh, well, of course I haven't told my colleagues here that you called me in to take a look at Dee. You asked me not to say anything."

"Not what I'm referring to, Dr. Neal, and I think you know it. I suppose we could call that some sort of cover-up, but it's certainly not worth worrying about. But you were more worried about other matters. Your visit to the library to examine the Prime Minister's body, for example."

"But ... I didn't ... I mean ..." Perry tailed off helplessly under the inspector's implacable gaze.

"You gave yourself away, Doctor," continued Constable. "You were a little too ready with the information when I asked you if you had seen Mrs. Ronson's body. No, you replied, however curious you might have been when you were first told. But there was just the tiniest pause before you came out with your denial. And when you examined Mrs. Nye, you gave your opinion that the death had only occurred a matter of minutes earlier ... 'this time'. Unlike the previous time you had examined a body, when it had been clear that the Prime Minister had been dead for some hours. So I think your curiosity overcame any other scruples. Although there is, of course, another more sinister explanation. Might you have wanted to check the scene of Mrs. Ronson's murder to make sure that you hadn't left any tell-tale evidence? And when we called you in to take a look at Mrs. Nye, was that fortuitous for you as it gave you the opportunity to do the same thing?"

"Yes. All right. I did leave my room and go down to the library," admitted Perry. "But it was completely innocent. Well, perhaps not ... more a case of plain human curiosity. I couldn't believe what Inspector Deare had told me. I had to see for myself. So I stole downstairs while she was in telling one of the others, but then I came back up again more or less straight away. In fact, I was lucky not to be seen, because she was just coming out of Benny's room. But that's all that happened. I didn't have any need to clear away incriminating evidence. Why on earth would I have wanted to kill Dee or Doris?"

"I'm afraid we're back to the matter of a cover-up, sir," said Constable. "You paid a visit to the church in Dammett Worthy on your way here, and we know about the conversations you had there, both with the vicar and with Mrs. Ronson. Piecing together the various scraps, it seems there was a case involving one of your patients, some years ago, where there was a death which could have been avoided if only you had taken other measures. But the potential scandal was covered up. It sounds as if this has continued to prey upon your mind. It also sounds as if, somehow, the details of the case became known to Mrs. Ronson, and might have been on the verge of becoming public. The Prime Minister couldn't risk leaving in place a Health Minister with such a question mark over his head. She might even have discussed the legal implications with her Justice Secretary. So, you see, any suspicions about yourself can be completely justified. And who better than a doctor to choose the particular method used - an injection - to bring about the death of Deborah Nye?"

Chapter 16

"Is this actually getting us anywhere, inspector?" Benjamin Fitt jumped to his feet and came forward to challenge the detective. "You're telling us all these things about people's backgrounds and stuff, giving away things which some of us probably thought were nobody's business but their own, and all this with a tabloid hack in the room who is probably rubbing his hands together at all the tasty copy he's going to get out of it. That book deal he talked about is going to be worth a mint. And you don't seem to be getting any closer to telling us who murdered Doris and Dee."

"All in good time, Mr. Fitt," responded Andy Constable. He checked his watch. "I think it's important that these facts should be gone over, and I'm not quite up against my deadline yet. And as for the matter of Mr. Daly, I think I'll be advising him to tread carefully in respect of the information that he reveals, particularly as we might be considering charges of impeding a police investigation and wasting police time if he steps over the line."

"Message received and understood, Mr. Constable," said Jim. "But I suspect we'll probably be having a little chat anyway when this is all over."

"I think you can count on it, Mr. Daly," said Constable. He turned back to Benny. "But in the meantime, let us carry on with our consideration of people's possible motives. And since you put yourself forward, Mr. Fitt, let's focus the spotlight on you."

"Focus away, inspector," replied Benny defiantly. "You won't find anything in my past career that's going to worry me. I'm not ashamed of anything I've done. My life is an open book."

"Maybe not quite that open, Mr. Fitt," demurred Constable. "Oh, I'm sure your parliamentary career, and your work in the trade unions before that, will bear the closest scrutiny."

"Well then?"

"But it's before that, in your younger years, that I suspect something has come back to haunt you. And it's not even the worst of secrets. You gave me a brief résumé of your life, but you skated over the matter of your up-bringing. 'I got out', you told me. But what you didn't mention was what you left behind. Except that you couldn't leave your past behind completely. And it's perhaps, for you, the most unfortunate of coincidences that the fellow M.P. you chose as your parliamentary assistant represents the constituency in which you grew up. Did you put him in place because of some sort of misplaced nostalgia about the old days?" A snort from Benny. "Well, perhaps not. You didn't display much nostalgia about them when you were speaking to me. But it appears that there was something to cause you concern, if what was overheard by several people is to be believed. For instance, when you were leaving the

Dammett Well, the landlord Mr. Porter witnessed an exchange between Mrs. Ronson and yourself which mentioned that assistant of yours and his constituency. A remarkable coincidence regarding the name of a lady living there who had come for him for help. There was a mention of close family relationships, and a determination to go over the matter in detail later. And this was after an initial conversation in the car on the way to the Inn, when Mr. Grade had heard much the same thing, speaking of the need to be above reproach. Which implies, of course, that reproaches were in order. So, Mr. Fitt, what conclusions am I to draw from the fact that one of Mr. Daly's press colleagues promised him 'the mother of all revelations'? Was that significant wording?"

There was a prolonged pause. "I never had a dad, you know," said Benny. He seemed far away. "Not that that was anything unusual on our estate. But most of the other boys had mothers who treated them like little princes. They had nothing, but they gave them everything. Not mine. She ... she was too busy with what she called my new uncles. She didn't care if they ... well, you don't need to know what it was like in our house. But if you knew, you wouldn't wonder why I got out. And I made up my mind I'd stay out. I was never going back, and I was never going to see ... that woman again. And then, suddenly, there I am in the government. I'm on the news. And she saw her chance to cash in. She got in touch, wanting this, wanting that. I said I'd have nothing to do with her. She said I'd better, otherwise she'd be on to the papers with stories about how I was a tearaway as a kid, got up to all sorts. And it was all nothing ... only stuff that all boys do, nothing serious, nothing criminal. But she started to put the whispers about. That could have been the end of me."

"And someone in that situation might have lashed out at the women who held his fate in their hands," suggested Constable softly.

"Which meant I killed Doris?" Benny gave a faint but pitying smile. "And that just goes to show you don't know a thing about her. And to be honest, neither did I. When I got called in last night, I was expecting the worst. I thought I was going to have my cards handed to me double quick. And she sat me down, told me what she had been told, and asked if I had anything to say. So I explained. The whole thing, chapter and verse, right from the beginning. I'd never been able to do that before, to anyone. It was a release. And she sat there for a minute, and then she came round the desk, put her arm around my shoulder, and said we would get me through it together. I couldn't believe it. She said she'd put her own enquiries in place, and once she had the facts, woe betide anyone who tried to get at me. They'd have to go through her first." Benny's voice began to shake, and he pulled out a handkerchief. "God, that woman was a real diamond." He took a deep breath, wiped his eyes, and drew himself up in his seat. "So, kill her, Mr.

Constable? I'd rather have killed anyone who tried."

"I think I'll choose not to hear that last statement, Mr. Fitt," said Constable. "The last thing I need is any further complication in this case."

"But couldn't that have meant he might have killed Dee?" pointed out Milo Grade. "Shouldn't you take him seriously? I mean, he might have killed her because he found out she'd murdered the Prime Minister. Although goodness knows why she would."

"Oh, there's a case to be made against Mrs. Nye, Mr. Grade. Not necessarily concerning the lady herself, but we've heard hints that her husband, who has considerable financial dealings at a high level, may not have been entirely ethical in all of them. Any suggestion of fraud in such elevated circles would be a very serious problem. There was a great deal of talk of fraud around the dinner table last night, and there would be nobody better placed to suppress any investigation than the wife of an accused person, if that wife happened to be the Justice Secretary. And no prime minister could continue to support the head of the legal system with such doubts hanging over her. But if the suggestion is that Mrs. Nye murdered this Prime Minister to protect herself, and then committed suicide in a fit of remorse, I have to tell you that the facts do not support such a theory, any more than they would support a suggestion of Mr. Fitt's involvement in Mrs. Nye's death."

"All your theories so far don't appear to be doing us much good," remarked Milo waspishly.

"Oh, never fear, Mr. Grade," replied Constable. "I have others. So, then, let me turn to you yourself."

"And what am I supposed to have done?" scoffed Milo. "Come on, let's hear what you've got to say about me."

"More a case of what you haven't done, Mr. Grade," responded the inspector. "In fact, it's almost the old 'the dog ate my homework' situation, which for an Education Secretary is very dangerous territory."

Milo blinked. "I have no idea what you're talking about."

"You were kind enough to tell me something about your background, sir. How you studied at university ... Politics, Philosophy, and Economics, I think you said ..." Constable ignored the small murmur of surprise from one corner of the room. "And with a grounding in these subjects, it's almost obligatory for a young man with ambition to take the first step on the road to a political career. First, as you explained, you were employed as a research assistant to an M.P., then you progressed to becoming an M.P. yourself, and now you find yourself with a seat around the Cabinet table. A very impressive career – almost textbook, one might say. But the only fly in the ointment is that the textbooks involved might not have been the right ones."

"This is meaningless," declared Milo. "It's all bluff."

"So it is, sir," said Constable. "But, unfortunately for you, not on my part. Because, as luck would have it, you came up against someone this weekend who could expose your bluff. Someone who recognised you from your university, but who certainly wouldn't have recognised your description of your studies. I have to be very grateful to Mr. Knightly for being in the right place at the right time. Because while he was on a hotel management course, one of the 'Foodies', as he described them, he saw you among the students on an engineering course. You were, in fact, one of the 'Spannermen'. And Spannermen, I'm guessing, do not generally emerge from their educational establishment with a First in P.P.E. So when you applied for that original job on an M.P.'s staff, it wasn't actually a case of the dog having eaten your homework, but the fact that there was no homework in the first place. Your qualifications were taken on trust, but they had been entirely fabricated."

"This is ridiculous," blustered Milo. "Even Doctor Johnson never finished his degree."

"That may be so, Mr. Grade, but as far as I'm aware, he never lied about it."

"You're guessing," retorted Milo. "You haven't a scrap of evidence. And how does this give me any reason to go around killing people?"

"You're right, Mr. Grade," said Constable. "A great deal of this is guesswork. But I can't tell you how many people have killed for motives far more trivial than these. You might well, for instance, have feared that, in the welter of revelations which seemed to be taking place, your secret had become known to the Prime Minister. You could have heard her in conversation with Mr. Knightly. I think, in the light of one of her remarks over dinner, you had every right to fear exposure and an end to your career. In any event, the question of school examination results was up for discussion. And so, as with so many of your colleagues here, a potential motive certainly exists."

Constable paused for several moments and took a pace or two up and down, as if marshalling his thoughts. "There's another way in which Mr. Knightly's evidence has been crucial in this investigation," he resumed, "but in this instance, it was not related to where he was and who he recognised, but rather the reverse."

"Sorry, inspector," said Phil, "but I don't understand. I think I've told you all I know."

"Forgive me, Mr. Knightly," said Constable. "I'm not explaining myself very well. I asked you if you knew any of those present in your hotel, and you said, personally, no. None of them had been here before, and you'd been on duty here ever since the establishment opened. Except, of course, that wasn't completely correct. You mentioned an absence over a weekend – your birthday, I think you said."

"Yes. I'd almost forgotten that. But it was only a couple of days."

"Quite enough to make a difference, sir. And as it happens, those couple of days were very important. Because, of course, even in your absence, the register continues to record the guests staying here. And that register was found in Mrs. Ronson's possession when we examined her room. Why, I wondered. I'm still not sure. But Sergeant Copper made a very interesting discovery when he went through it." Constable's gaze swept around the room. "The fact is, one of you had stayed here before. Almost exactly a year ago. It so happens, Mr. Knightly, that that visit coincided with your birthday, which is why you didn't recognise the hotel's former guest. Who had, I assume, come here to celebrate a special occasion at the same date. Her and her husband's anniversary. Am I right, Mrs. Hayste?"

Marion looked momentarily disconcerted, but then her face cleared. "Do you know, Mr. Constable, you're absolutely right. We did come here for a little break over our anniversary weekend. But we often go away for weekends, so it must have slipped my mind. There's surely nothing strange in that." She attempted a light laugh.

"Indeed not, Mrs. Hayste. Except that you told me that you'd never been here before. A simple lapse of memory? Perhaps. Although I would have thought that a weekend spent in the luxurious surroundings of His Lordship's Room, as the register shows, would have stuck in your mind. And you were almost too eager to point out that you had never been inside the room, currently occupied by Dr. Neal. I'm afraid that we were initially slightly misled by your fluttered reaction, and the fact that there was a concealed communicating door between your room and his, and we began to draw an incorrect conclusion."

"What's that you say?" Perry Neal gave the inspector an enquiring look. "What, you mean that you thought Marion and I ...?" He gave a 'tcha' of annoyance. "For goodness sake, man, I'm old enough to be her father."

"But, as I say," continued Constable, declining to be diverted, "that supposition was incorrect. But if that wasn't the cause of Mrs. Hayste's unease, then what was? And once we began to put together the different pieces of the jigsaw, a picture began to emerge. There were the various overheard remarks. Mr. Knightly walked in on a heated conversation between Mrs. Hayste and Mrs. Nye, purportedly on the subject of one of her areas of ministerial responsibility. 'Marion and drugs' – those were the words used to me. The question of the use of drugs in prisons – or was it perhaps more a case of drugs being allowed to get into prisons through inefficiencies in the regime? Mrs. Ronson spoke of 'watering down' – so was it simple inefficiency, or was there a hint of corruption? But why should a minister be open to such a thing? Let me offer a wild speculation. Could it be that the person who was supposed to be the gamekeeper was in fact one of the poachers? A user? Perhaps with access to a hypodermic syringe? A syringe which was subsequently used as a murder weapon? I don't suppose, Mrs. Hayste, that you'd care to raise the sleeves of the dress you're wearing so that we may take a closer look at your arms?"

Marion remained seated and silent, absolutely still save for a slight tremor in her hands. Her blue eyes, with their black dilated pupils, were fixed on the inspector's face.

After a few moments' pause, Constable resumed. "And we mustn't, of course, forget the other murder weapon – the one which was used to kill Mrs. Ronson. A knife taken from the desk of the hotel manager, Mr. Knightly. But Mr. Knightly's office is tucked away behind hidden doorways, and not obviously accessible. Except, of course, to one who knows the secrets of the servants' staircases and the concealed entrances. Someone who would know how to move about the building without encountering the other guests.

"So, to recap, we have a guest who denies having visited the hotel before. Why would she do that? We have a minister whose performance of her duties is failing to find favour not only with her departmental superior, but also her ultimate boss, the Prime Minister. Is dismissal the least of her worries, or is she facing something worse? And in her agitated state, does she seek to protect herself by removing the two people who threaten her? And does she use the means which she happens to have at her immediate disposal? A syringe from which we have obtained a clear and conclusive set of fingerprints." Constable waited. There was a very long silence, which none of those in the room seemed disposed to break. Eventually, the inspector spoke again. "Well, Mrs. Hayste? Is there anything you wish to say?"

Dave Copper stepped forward. "Sir, I don't want to speak out of turn, but are you sure? I mean, shouldn't we ..."

"Caution me?" interrupted Marion. A slow smile of surprising sweetness stole over her features. "Oh sergeant, I think it's all a little too late for that." She took a very deep breath and gave a long sigh. "And I think I owe it to my colleagues here to tell the whole truth, especially in view of what I suspect they're all going to have to go through in the aftermath of this." She looked Constable directly in the eye. "And I owe it to you too, inspector. You may have worked out the truth about what has happened, but you must still be wondering about one or two things regarding the how and why.

"It's ironic, really. I mean, that the Prime Minister should appoint me to a position with responsibility for the drugs regime in prisons. I wish I could say that I'm alone in my generation in having a relationship with drugs, but that would be dishonest. Society may disapprove in principle, but the number of people who find themselves in my situation might very well surprise you. Media people, sports personalities, stars in show business, politicians – the list is endless. Including my husband. He started off supplying me with what I needed, and in the end I convinced myself that I loved him for it, and I married him. I thought he had the means to make me happy. Recreational use, it's called. Nothing harmful, they say. It's nobody's business but your own. Until, that is, you find yourself in the public spotlight. And what could be more public than being placed at the head of a headline campaign to tackle the problem in some of the state's institutions? Could I have been any more vulnerable to blackmail? But the people I was tangled up with weren't after money. In fact, you might say they were very generous to me. But in return, they wanted their lives made easier, and the drugs trade into prisons is big business. So I was trapped.

"I don't know how Dee found out." Marion shrugged. "It's enough that she did, and she was determined that the Prime Minister had to know. I suppose I can't really blame her for that. And when the P.M. called me in, she demanded the full story, chapter and verse. She made me write everything down in a resignation letter – names, dates, places – all the information that I had about the people who were at the heart of the business. So when I went up to bed, I knew that it was the end of everything. I even thought of doing away with myself. After all, I had the means – a simple overdose, and that would be an end to it. I expect you'll be searching my room, inspector – you'll find all the evidence you need there, with the exception of that one syringe you already have. But I didn't have the courage to do anything. And then the idea came into my head – that letter I'd written for the Prime Minister was as good as my death warrant anyway. These were very dangerous people. I felt I must get it back. I thought I could persuade her into giving it back to me. So I went down the servants' staircase and into the office – that's where I saw the knife. And I thought, if persuasion doesn't work, I'll have to try threats. I must have been mad. I even tried to buy the P.M.'s mercy by telling her the full story of Dee's husband and her cover-up of his dealings. But of course, as always, Doris was adamant. She turned her back on me in contempt – and before I realised what I was doing, she was lying dead on the floor with the knife in her back. I tried to wipe the handle clean with a napkin that was on the desk, and that's when I saw my letter still lying there. I took it and came back upstairs the way I'd come. I burnt it in the grate in my room."

With a sudden shriek of rage, Erica launched herself at Marion. But swift as she was, Dave Copper's reactions were just as rapid, and he managed to intercept the furious minister before the outstretched fingernails could inflict any damage on her intended victim. There was a moment's confusion as everyone reacted in shock and horror, while Erica writhed, spitting incoherently in Copper's grasp, before subsiding just as quickly as she had erupted. Gently, the sergeant forced the now limp and sobbing minister back into her armchair, while Constable nodded an instruction to Una Singleton, and the two junior officers took up station on either side of Erica.

"I think we may all understand your

reaction, Ms. Mayall," said Constable calmly, "given the nature of your feelings for Mrs. Ronson. But I'm sure you would rather leave it to others to ensure that justice takes its course in this case." He held Erica's eyes until she, with a visible effort to master herself, gave a mute nod. "And besides, there are still some details to reveal." He turned back to Marion, who had remained transfixed at the suddenness of the attack. "Mrs. Hayste?"

"What is it they say in 'Macbeth'?" murmured Marion unexpectedly, gazing unfocussed above the heads of the others. "Something about killing being easier once you've started?" She looked at Constable. "It's true, inspector. I was horrified at what I'd done. Horrified, but still terrified. I may have recovered the letter and destroyed it, but Dee still knew everything. I was twisting and turning in my mind, but in the end I decided that the only way to prevent her telling what she knew was to kill her. So I took my syringe and I went to her room. She was lying on her bed, half-asleep. Before she'd even woken properly, I'd held her and injected her." Suddenly, all Marion's composure deserted her, and the tears began to flow. "And now I wish I'd had the courage to use it on myself." She collapsed weeping against the inspector.

Andy Constable, after a few moments, handed over the now exhausted Marion into the care of Sheila Deare, who had stepped forward during the final revelations. "I think that is perhaps enough information for the present. Inspector Deare, if you would escort Mrs. Hayste outside, Sergeant Copper will make the necessary arrangements for taking her into custody." He looked around the drawing room at the congregation of politicians, still sitting stunned and silent at what had occurred. "And now, if you will excuse me, ladies and gentlemen, I have a very important phone call to Downing Street to make." He glanced at his watch. "And only five minutes to make it." He strode from the room, his police colleagues and their charge following in his wake.

The Final Chapter

"So you were caught up in all that?" marvelled Sergeant Pete Radley. "And for two weeks since, you haven't said a word."

"Sorry, guys," said Dave Copper, perched on the edge of his desk. "Sworn to secrecy, and all that."

"What, with the Prisons Minister under arrest?" said Pete. "That's what the rumour is. And my spies reckon that you were the one who actually slammed the cuffs on. So what's that all about?"

Copper pulled a face and shook his head mutely.

"Come on, mate," coaxed Constable Matt Cawston. "Those were some pretty high-powered people. There's got to be something you can tell us. What goes on behind the scenes in the corridors of power, and all that."

Copper shrugged. "Would if I could, chaps, but it can't be done. I am under strict instructions from on high not to utter a single syllable about the whole business, and certainly not before it comes to court. So you can beg and plead all you like, but you ain't getting anywhere."

"Yes, but look," persisted Pete. "Three of the Cabinet have resigned already, and that's before the new prime minister is even officially in place. You can't tell me that's a coincidence. 'Spending more time with their families', indeed!" he scoffed. "We've all heard that one. That just means that there are some juicy secrets waiting to get out, and they're jumping before they're pushed. And I bet you know what they're hiding."

"More than my job's worth, guys." Copper was adamant. "And if you were in my shoes, you'd be doing exactly the same as me."

"I'll tell you one thing," said Matt. "I reckon I ought to put in for a transfer to C.I.D. double quick. It seems to me that you blokes on the detecting side get a lot more fun than us poor Joes stuck in the control room."

"Do it," encouraged Copper. "If being dragged out of bed by a phone call at three in the morning to go and look at some poor bedraggled corpse being hauled out of a muddy ditch is your idea of fun, I wouldn't stand in your way." He paused and smiled reflectively. "Actually, I wouldn't have had it any other way. But I suppose everything has to change eventually."

"How do you mean?" asked Pete.

"Oh, nothing much," replied Copper airily. "Just a random thought."

"You're getting very tight-lipped in your old age," complained Pete with a smile. "Secret thoughts, and you won't even chuck us a bone with the slightest sniff of a hint about the biggest case you've ever been involved in."

"Which just goes to prove that I'm not as daft as some people might think," retorted Copper with an answering grin. "You know very well that the guv would have my hide if he even knew we were having this conversation. So you'd better skedaddle double quick, before he catches you and me."

"By the way, where is he?" enquired Matt. "I haven't seen him around much lately. Is he taking some time off? Have the worthy citizens of the county suddenly stopped murdering people?"

"If only," said Copper. "Although actually, it has gone a bit quiet, thank goodness. I dare say everybody is too busy sitting at home watching all the loony speculation on the news to think about doing anything themselves. But as for the guv, he's about. In fact, he was in first thing this morning, probably before you two had even started ploughing your way through your bacon sarnies in the canteen, but then he scooted off to London."

"London? What's he up to up there? Here, it's all on top of this case, isn't it?" surmised Pete.

"Couldn't tell you," said Copper. "And before you have another go at me, that doesn't mean I won't tell you. It actually means I can't, because I don't know. He keeps getting mysterious calls from he-won't-tell-me-who, and then before I know it, he's disappeared in the direction of London. So your guess is as good as mine. But he said he'd be back this afternoon ..." Copper consulted his watch. "Probably sometime about now, so you two might want to get back to the control room, instead of hanging around here while Matt practises his interrogation techniques on me."

The suggestion came just a fraction too late. Footsteps could be heard approaching along the corridor, and Andy Constable appeared in the doorway to his office. A silence fell as Copper slid off the front of his desk, while his two friends came to an almost guilty state of attention.

"Good afternoon, gentlemen." The amusement was plainly audible in Constable's voice. "I seem to be interrupting something."

"Afternoon, sir," chorused the two visiting police officers.

"Anything we can do for you?"

"No, sir," said Pete. "We just popped in for a chat with Dave, you know, to ... er ..."

"... fix up another day to go to the races together," finished Matt hastily. "On account of him being so good at picking winners last time."

"And that's a talent which I'm sure won't be going to waste in the future," replied Constable with a quirky smile. "But in the meantime, my bet is that you three are going to find a more suitable time and place to sort out your social diary. Yes?"

"Er ... yes, sir. Of course, sir. Well, we'll ... er ..." With relief, the two uniformed officers escaped into the corridor, as Copper made a brave show of occupying himself with arranging the papers on his desk.

"Back then, guv," remarked the sergeant, somewhat unnecessarily.

"But not for long," said Constable, subsiding into the chair behind his desk with a deep sigh and checking his watch. "I have an appointment to go and see the Chief Constable in about half an hour, so that I can bring him up to date with what's been going on."

"Really?" Copper sounded intrigued. "Reports direct to the top brass, eh? You're moving in lofty circles these days, guv."

The inspector laughed softly. "Ain't that the truth?"

"So come on, sir," said Copper, leaning forward expectantly. "Spare a thought for a poor confused sergeant, and fill me in with what's been going on. You keep disappearing, and I'm getting questions from all sorts of people as to what actually went on at Dammett Hall."

"Including, no doubt, your gambling buddies."

"Don't worry, guv. I didn't say a thing. I know when to keep my mouth shut."

"Not necessarily true in all cases, David," smiled Constable. "The Copper sense of humour has always had a tendency to escape if it's not watched carefully. But when it matters, then yes, I know I can trust you."

The sergeant coloured slightly. "Thanks for that, guv. So ..." He raised interrogative eyebrows.

"Shut the door." Copper jumped to comply. "Just to confirm, this conversation is not taking place. So, where do you want to start?"

"Well, the Dammett Hall murders, of course, guv. There's hardly been a peep in the papers or on the news about the actual case. So, what's the score?"

"We've had the assistance of some very helpful and considerate editors, apparently. It was felt that, under the circumstances, the last thing the country needs is another huge flood of uncertainty, so everything is being kept as low-key as possible."

"But it's going to come to a trial, surely, sir?"

"Of course. And in order to make things quicker and easier, Marion Hayste will of course be pleading guilty. She says that's the least she can do to put an end to the matter."

"You've seen her?"

"Actually, yes."

"That's not normal, is it, guv?"

"Not really, but it was her idea. She asked specifically if I would go and visit her, so I could hardly refuse."

"What did she have to say?"

"Not that much, to be honest. She's feeling a lot of remorse. She takes full responsibility for what she did, but I think she wanted me to accept that, at heart, she wasn't a bad person. She wanted to explain how she let herself be trapped into doing what she did. And she blames herself for being taken in by that husband of hers and drawn into the whole drugs situation. Said she should never have rushed into marriage with him. He, by the way, is also now languishing in a cell somewhere, facing a number of other charges which could well see him being kept off the streets for a very long time."

"Her too, guv," mused Copper. "And it's

probably going to be even harder for her. I mean, he'll probably end up in prison with a load of drug-dealing soul-mates who'll think he's some kind of hero. But she ... well, she was the Prisons Minister, for goodness sake. Can you imagine how the other inmates are going to treat her? Even if she did bump off a couple of other politicians, which some people would probably want to thank her for. And it's not as if she'll be going down for five minutes, is it?"

"Indeed not. I suspect she may well opt for voluntary solitary confinement, which has its own drawbacks. But at least she'll have plenty of leisure to repent." A sigh. "Well, it'll be all up to the courts. Our job there is more or less done."

"Which still leaves me wondering, sir, how to account for the fact that you have been rather mysterious about these trips of yours to London. You haven't been spending all your time prison-visiting, surely?"

"No," admitted Constable. "As it happens, I had to ... pop into Downing Street."

"Pop into?" spluttered Copper incredulously. "You don't just 'pop into' Downing Street. They have things like security and screening, which I bet are going to be red hot at the moment. So what was that all about?"

Constable drew a breath. "Actually, it was the Security people I was going to see. I had to meet them."

"What, Inspector Deare's mob? And how is she getting along? I bet it's not been easy for her either."

"Oh, she's not too bad. She's holding things together until her replacement is in position."

"She did reckon she wouldn't be staying in the job long after what had happened, didn't she, guv?"

"She did indeed. And she wasn't wrong. But then I got called in to see the Deputy P.M. - although actually, I suppose we now have to call him the caretaker Prime Minister until the new P.M. is officially appointed. But the word is that his path is being smoothed in the interests of continuity, and nobody is going to stand against him, so it'll all be cut and dried within the next couple of days."

"And then he'll be looking for someone to replace Inspector Deare as his Head of Security, eh?"

"Well, actually, no." Constable took a very deep breath and let out a long sigh. "He's already found someone." A lengthy pause. "Me."

Dave Copper's jaw literally dropped open in amazement. "You, guv?" He recovered himself. "Bloody hell! That's fantastic!" He leapt up and pumped his colleague's hand. "That's brilliant! But how ... why ... I mean, when ...?"

"Apparently some very complimentary things have been said about me behind the scenes by all manner of people," said Constable. "And Downing Street were keen to have a new pair of eyes to take a fresh look at things, from outside the existing apparatus. My name cropped up, and it seems to have snowballed from there. As for when, more or less immediate effect.

That's the news I'm about to go and impart to the Chief Constable. Transfer to the Met ... promotion to the rank of Commander ..." He shook his head disbelievingly. "It's all happening."

Copper subsided back into his chair. "We're going to miss you, guv. I'm ... going to miss you. That's going to change everything for me too, isn't it?" His face wore a concerned frown. "Have you got any idea who I'm going to be working for after you've gone?"

Constable laughed. "Fretting about continuing to be a poor confused sergeant after my departure, eh? To be honest, David, I think that's the least of your worries. But if I can offer you a word of advice, I think you ought to check your inbox rather more frequently."

"Eh?" In puzzlement, Copper turned to the laptop on his desk and clicked a few keys.

"I think keeping yourself up to speed is going to take a very much higher priority from now on, Mr. Copper."

Copper, intent on his screen, started to scroll through his emails. "Mostly the usual dross, guv ... oh, hang on, there's one here from ..." He opened the message, and the frown on his face was slowly replaced by a beaming grin of delight. "It's here ... I've ... I've got it!"

"Oh yes? And what would that be?" enquired Constable, making an unsuccessful attempt to stifle a smile. "Something you want to tell me?"

"I passed, guv," glowed the sergeant. "I got

the promotion. They're making me up to Detective Inspector." He broke off and cast an accusing glance at his fellow-officer. "You knew, didn't you, guv? When? Why didn't you say something?"

"I only found out first thing this morning," replied Constable. "They copied the notification to me for information. But what with one thing and another, I haven't really had the opportunity to mention it since, have I? Plus I didn't want to spoil your pleasure in the discovery. Anyway, congratulations. It's well-deserved."

"Wow." Copper sat back in his chair. "D.I. Copper," he marvelled. "Doesn't sound too bad, does it, guv?"

"I think we might all get used to it eventually," smiled Constable. "Oh, by the way, less of the 'guv' from now on, if you don't mind. If we're going to be the same rank ... well, for a little while, anyway ... you're going to have to make it 'Andy' from now on. Eh, David?"

"Righty-ho, guv ... er ... Andy. Although it's going to feel a bit weird to start with. I might have to hark back to the arrangement we had when we were in Spain and call you 'A.C.'"

"Better not do that when I'm with the Met," chuckled Constable. "The Assistant Commissioner might suspect that I have unworthy ambitions." He glanced at the wall clock. "And now I had better make my way in the direction of the Chief Constable to break the glad tidings to him. About the fact that he's got a ready-made replacement for me when I've gone,

I mean," he added with a smile, uncoiling himself from behind his desk. "If you want to try out this chair for size while I'm away, feel free."

"All change, then, sir ... Andy."

"As you say, all change." Constable halted with his hand on the doorknob. "Oh, by the way, that name. You might have wondered about it, over the years."

Copper shrugged. "Not really, guv. How do you mean?"

"It must have crossed your mind that, every time somebody wanted to call me 'Andrew', I put them right and insisted on 'Andy'."

"Never really gave it a thought, guv. I just thought it was one of those things."

"And a fine detective inspector you'll make if you don't sharpen up those inquisitive skills," remarked Constable in mock severity. "But I think you've earned the right to be let into this little guilty secret of mine."

Copper looked dubious. "We've had a bucketful of guilty secrets in our time, guv. Are you sure I need to know this one?"

"Need to? No. But I think you'll enjoy it. Call it my present to you in celebration of your promotion."

"Okay. Go on." Copper still sounded doubtful.

"You remember that story about the footballer and his snooty wife? How they were on a trip overseas, and it so happened that she got pregnant during their travels, and they named their son after the place where they reckoned he was conceived?"

"Y-e-e-s."

"Well, they weren't the first to have the idea. When my parents got married, in the year you need not trouble to work out, they didn't have a great deal of money, so they couldn't afford a honeymoon abroad. They were too busy getting the cash together to set up home. But they did manage to have a few days away together in a lovely little old-fashioned pub, not totally different from the Dammett Well Inn, in the Hampshire countryside, very close to a market town. Want to take a guess at the name of the town?"

Copper racked his brains for a few moments. "Not ... oh, you're kidding!"

"That's right, David. The name of the town was Andover."

After a few moments of silence, all those working in offices further along the corridor were startled by the sound of prolonged and uproarious male laughter.

*   *   *

The Inspector Constable Murder Mysteries

Murderer's Fête
Who could have foreseen the murder of a clairvoyant at a country house fête?

Murder Unearthed
Sun, sangria and suspects during a supposed holiday in Spain

Death Sails In The Sunset
Murder ensues when a journalist refuses to let guilty secrets be buried at sea

Murder Comes To Call
Three short stories to tax the talents of our detectives

Murder Most Frequent
Another trilogy of intriguing cases for Constable and Copper

The Odds On Murder
Someone is riding for a fall when a prominent racehorse trainer is killed

The Murder Cabinet
A return to Dammett Hall leaves the fate of the nation in the team's hands

All titles available worldwide from Amazon on Kindle and in paperback

Printed in Great Britain
by Amazon